DANCING THROUGH LIFE
BOOK FOUR

AN IRISH
Slip Step

PATRICIA M. ROBERTSON

"Your feet will bring you to where your heart is."

Chapter 1

The young woman stared out the cracked window of the Brooklyn walk-up as flakes of falling snow melted on the ledge and streets below. She pushed back a strand of hair from her face and placed her hand on her expanding waist.

How did she get here? This was not the life she had envisioned when she first came to New York. Then she had been sure her dreams were about to come true. She would work hard until she was discovered and pulled from the chorus line into stardom. She had joined the ranks of so many young people, auditioning for parts, working as a waitress, waiting for the magical break-through.

So far, over the past five years, she had been in two touring companies and three Broadway productions but never made it beyond the chorus line. Now, her dancing days were over, at least until after the birth of her baby.

She didn't know why she kept the baby. The father was another acting hopeful, currently on the road and barely able to support himself. She had considered an abortion. Her friends had encouraged her to do this.

"A baby will change everything. You won't be able to support yourself. You won't be able to tour with a baby. You'll never make it," they told her.

She had thought about it, but it never seemed like the right time so she kept putting it off until it was too late. Another decision made by default, she told herself. She couldn't bring herself to do it, even though she hadn't embraced motherhood either. So here she was, five months away from giving birth. She wasn't ready.

"Couldn't you give me more time, God? More time to make it as a star? Then I could quit for a while in order to focus on motherhood," she prayed, but God didn't answer. Or if He did, she couldn't hear Him. She was running out of time.

She looked at the small Christmas tree sitting on the end table in the corner of the one bedroom apartment she shared with another acting hopeful. The one bedroom had been converted into a two bedroom by portioning off part of the living room, providing some small semblance of privacy. The tree was the only acknowledgement of the season she had allowed herself. Under its bare branches was a simple crèche, Mary, Joseph and a baby.

"How did you do it?' Chloe asked the small statuette in blue. "You weren't married when you were pregnant, but at least you had Joseph, and you had other family members. I have no one. How can I do it?" She regretted her decision not to decide about an abortion. "It seems I've been drifting through life. How can I raise a child by myself? A baby changes everything," she repeated the words of her friends.

"You can give the baby up for adoption," one of her fellow aspiring actors had suggested. "Lose your baby fat and you can be back on the circuit in a few months. There are even people willing to pay all your expenses and more for a healthy baby."

Chloe had ignored that suggestion as well. So here she was with growing debt and only her waitress tips and wages to pay the bills.

Could she go home, she wondered. She looked at her phone. Her parents were just a call away, or were they? Would they welcome their prodigal daughter? She had not left on good terms, had not kept in touch. Could she show up now, take the bus back home? Mary had made the trip to Bethlehem while pregnant with Jesus. Maybe she could do it too. All she need do is pick up the phone, call her parents and get on the bus.

Chloe stared at the phone, then dialed the number of the one person she knew she could count on.

"Grandpa?"

Chapter 2

Howard put the phone back down and scratched his head. Was this real? Sometimes the line between reality and memories blurred. Had his granddaughter really called him, or had he imagined it?

He had been startled awake by the sound of the phone ringing. Who would be calling at this time of night, he had wondered as he glanced at his watch. Only nine o'clock. He had fallen asleep in front of the TV, the way he did most nights. He had come home from the Christmas recital at the dance center, fixed himself something to eat, and promptly fell asleep in his reclining rocker. He shook his head and pushed himself out of the lounge chair as he tried to remember where he had left his phone. The sound seemed to be coming from the kitchen.

"Hello," he had cleared his throat to shake the sleep from his voice.

"Grandpa?"

"Chloe?"

"Grandpa, can I come home?"

"What do you mean? To your mom and dad's?"

"No, to your house. You and Grandma were always home to me."

"Where are you?"

"New York. I'm in trouble."

"What kind of trouble?" Howard sat down, preparing for whatever would come next.

There was silence on the line then the voice saying, "I'm pregnant."

This time it was Howard's turn to be silent.

"Grandpa, you still there?"

"Of course you can come, baby. You are always welcome. Do you need money?"

"No, I've got enough to take the bus." It had been settled.

What would Helen have done, he wondered. She probably would have slapped Chloe on the side of her head then given her a big hug. That was her way.

Chloe's voice had sounded so like Helen's. At first he had thought it was Helen, Helen as he remembered her, as his young bride.

Sometimes it seemed as if she were talking to him. Helen was more real to him than the shadows that haunted his dreams. She wasn't a shadow. She was more than a memory. She was his flesh and blood, a part of him. The life they had shared together was more real than the life he lived now.

It was a good life. He had made new friends. Still he came home alone to the new house they had bought just as Helen's Alzheimer's was becoming more apparent. The memories here were not the ones he wanted to remember. He remembered those early days of their courtship, how they had met in Ireland at the end of World War II.

He had enlisted as soon as he had turned eighteen. His mother had wanted him to finish high school first, but he had been afraid he would miss all the action if he did that. After what the Japanese had done to them at Pearl Harbor, he had wanted to get some Japs. Instead he had been sent to Ireland, just in time for VE Day, had spent a few months there and had been preparing with the rest of the base to go to the Pacific when Truman had dropped the bomb on Hiroshima and Nagasaki ending the war. He had missed his chance he had thought, feeling guilty as he listened to the tales of others who had fought in the war. Feeling guilty, as he was applauded as a veteran when he had not seen combat. He had returned home after his tour of duty, finished up high school and went on to college on the GI bill, becoming a mechanical engineer, but not before falling in love with the fair Helen.

They had sent letters back and forth across the Atlantic. She had only been sixteen when they had met, too young to marry, and so their long distance courtship continued through his years in college until he was finally able to bring her home and start their life together.

Chapter 3

Northern Ireland – 1945

"Get up, lazy," Brigid yanked the covers off of her sister. "We have chores to get done." Mary Helen rolled over, reaching for the covers.

"Let me sleep," she moaned.

"You aren't getting away with that. If we don't finish our chores, there'll be no going to the celebration this afternoon."

What celebration, Mary Helen wondered? Then she remembered. The war was over! There was going to be a parade and dancing! She loved dancing. She jumped out of the bed she shared with her sister. How could she have forgotten? Soon her brothers would be home, especially Jimmy, her favorite brother. Liam had been too full of his own self-importance to pay any attention to his little sister. Jimmy was the one who had watched out for her at school. Jimmy was the one who had taught her which neighborhoods to avoid and how to take care of herself.

"Girls need to know how to fight, too," he had told her as he showed her how to lay a punch on an unsuspecting victim. She couldn't wait to see him again.

Her grandmother's bed was already empty. Granny always got up early to start the fire, warm the house and cook the breakfast porridge. It was her morning ritual, one she had done every morning of Mary Helen's life that she remembered.

Mary Helen dressed in her work clothes and hurried down the steps to the cozy kitchen. A pot of porridge sat on the stove. The fire in the fireplace had chased away the morning dampness.

"Looks to be a beautiful day, once the clouds break," said her grandfather, her mum's dad, sitting at the table reading the morning paper. Granny was her dad's mum. Both had lost their spouses years ago. They tolerated each other, as if they had been married, getting along for the sake of a place to stay. Granda Mike was no longer able to trek up and down the stairs and so slept on a cot in the living room. There were two bedrooms upstairs, the one occupied by her parents and the one that had once held the whole brood of five, plus a small room barely big enough for a twin bed that had formerly housed

Granda Mike. The three oldest had since moved on; Margaret, the oldest, was married with children of her own, Liam and Jimmy were fighting in France. Then there was Brigid and Mary Helen. Mary Helen was the youngest of the five.

"It will rain like every day in Ireland, you old sot." Granny responded to Granda Mike's optimism with her characteristic will to fight.

"Do you think the rain will hold off till the washing is dry?" Mary Helen asked. It fell to her and Brigid to do the family washing each week.

"Likely it will rain while you are at your parade, leaving me to bring it all in," Granny complained.

"You're coming with us, aren't you Granny? You don't want to miss the feis," Brigid asked. Mary Helen was aware that Brigid knew the answer to her question, but, always the peacemaker, Brigid felt she had to ask anyway.

"The witch won't leave her lair," Granda Mike taunted.

"Hush, Granda. It's a day for celebrating. Must you start so early?" Brigid intervened. For her part, Mary Helen enjoyed the quarrels. It was entertainment.

"We'll have the washing done and put away before we go," Brigid assured her grandmother. "Mary Helen, we must get started. Don't dawdle."

Her parents had already left for work. The war had been a boon to Northern Ireland manufacturing. Her mom had a job as a clerk for a boat manufacturer. Her dad, a former merchant marine, worked as a cook at a hotel. He had been called in early to help with the breakfast shift. Both would be off work in time for the parade. Everyone had been given the afternoon off to celebrate.

As Mary Helen washed the clothes, she day-dreamed. No more rationing, she dreamed. All of the eggs and meat she could eat. And butter! How was one to get by on one pat of butter a week? And she could have nylon stockings. No more air raids or war drills. Finally there would be peace. She couldn't imagine what that would be like.

She loved to listen to her grandfather's stories at night. As he told it, there had never been peace in Ireland. Theirs was a history of war and fighting. Barbarians over-running the country, invasions by the Brits and English rule, the IRA and Sinn Fein and the fight for freedom from England. Even with the establishment of the Republic of Ireland in 1921 this battle had not ended entirely as there was still interference by the British in Irish affairs in the southern part of the island and calls for a united Ireland, north and south. The six counties of Northern Ireland had remained under British Rule through political maneuvering.

The sense of betrayal felt by both of her remaining grandparents was still strong over twenty years since the split. Granny's husband had been active in the resistance and died during the Anglo-Irish war for freedom. Granny remained an active member of the IRA, though not as actively as in the past. Mary Helen remembered strange men coming and going at night, midnight meetings that she was not supposed to know about.

As part of Britain, Northern Ireland was a staging area for troops coming and going into battle. Belfast was also hit by air raids during the early years of the war. They had not been bombed for the past year, still the fear remained.

"We're neither fish nor fowl," her granny would complain about their state. "We aren't British, but we also aren't free Irish. We are stuck between the two."

Her parents seemed okay with British rule, or at least not as opposed as her grandparents. They realized there were some benefits with being connected to England. They were to be treated as English citizens and so enjoyed services provided by the English government, something which the poor in the Republic of Ireland lacked. Politicians in the free Republic spoke against such welfare benefits. There were benefits, however most of those benefits went to the Prods. Catholics were still treated like second class citizens, trapped by laws aimed to keep them in poverty.

Mary Helen wasn't concerned about politics. She was more concerned about being allowed to attend local dances. These had been curtailed by the war and curfews. Now that the war was over, Mary Helen looked forward to being able to go out at night, tagging along with her sister, Brigid.

It turned out to be a glorious day. The clouds lifted, leaving the city awash in sunshine. There were American soldiers everywhere, joining in the festivities. Mary Helen pulled her auburn hair up in a ribbon, put on her best dress, and followed Brigid to the town center where she met her friends from school. She left Brigid behind as she went off, arm in arm with her friends. At the town center, an impromptu band began to play. She kicked off her shoes and joined other dancers on the green, holding hands with her friends as they danced a step dance in a circle. When the music shifted to a slip jig, she let go of her friends' hands, dropped her arms to her side as she kicked and whirled about the green, laughing as her hair pulled loose from the ribbon. A group of American soldiers gathered to watch. They applauded as she finished. Mary Helen blushed, did a quick curtsy, tied her hair back up and joined her friends, avoiding any attempt by the soldiers to talk to her.

It had been a grand day. Mary Helen reluctantly returned home for supper, hoping to go out again that night. She was surprised by a crowd gathered in the living room. The sounds of her mother and grandmother's wails met her at the door.

"What has happened?" she asked.

Her aunt took her aside into the kitchen. "Your brother, Jimmy. He didn't make it."

"But that's not possible. The war is over."

"They just identified his body. It was in the final offensive he was killed." Mary Helen sat in shock. Her glorious day, how could it have ended like this?

Chapter 4

"I can't believe I ever thought I could have a relationship with a minister," Kathleen mumbled under her breath as she came into the kitchen.

"What, dear, did you say something?" Esther asked. Kathleen was surprised to see her up.

"Nothing, Mom. What are you doing up?"

"Just getting a glass of water. Is something wrong?"

"I'm fine, Mom. Go back to bed." As fine as a forty-year-old still living with her mother can be, she said to herself. She couldn't believe she had ever thought she could date a minister and she couldn't believe she was still living in her mother's house, and now with a stepfather.

"What's going on?" That's all she needed, Peter questioning her, too. "I heard voices and thought I should check it out."

"Shhhh, just Kathleen getting home from her date. Don't wake up Dad or Scott." That would be the full complement of family, her grandfather and her son, four generations living under one roof. Could it get any worse?

"How was your date?"

It just got worse.

"I'm going to bed." Kathleen made a hasty retreat to her basement room. At least it afforded her some semblance of privacy. The last thing she wanted to do was talk about her date.

"What would be so bad about you coming to the Christmas Eve service? It is Christmas, after all. My parents will be visiting. They want to meet you," Joe had insisted.

"Because I don't do church. You knew that when I started dating you. Why should that change now?"

"Because it's Christmas. What would one service hurt?"

"And meet all those church members?"

"They would like to meet you."

"And then it would be Easter, and someone's baptism, and church socials. I don't want to get roped into any of that."

"You knew I was a minister when we started dating. This is my life. It's not going to change."

"I'm not the one asking you to change. You are asking me to change."

"I thought that . . ." Joe shook his head and stopped.

"You thought what? That I would change?"

"I thought that, after Joy's death and the events of last year, that, yes, that maybe since you are no longer angry with God, that maybe you would start to come to church."

"God and I are okay. That doesn't mean I have to go to church."

"No, but I thought . . ."

"You thought I would become one of your church members, your 'sheep,' and quietly get in line."

"I don't expect you to do anything quietly."

"Then what do you expect?"

Joe took a deep breathe, "Church is an important part of my life. I would like to be able to share that with you."

"Is that the case, or am I an embarrassment to you? How can you, the minister, be involved with someone who doesn't go to any church? Well, I'll solve that problem for you. We are done. Take me home." Kathleen sat without speaking during the drive home, afraid of what she would say if she spoke.

Joe appeared calm as he stared ahead into the darkness. "So, I guess this is it," he said as he parked in her driveway.

"Yes, it is."

"So, I'll see you around," Joe said, not giving her their customary kiss, not shaking her hand, just staring ahead.

"Yeah, sure, see ya." Not if I see you first, Kathleen thought as she slid out the door and into the kitchen. The last thing she wanted was a heart-to-heart with her mom.

"I have to get a place of my own," was her last thought as she fell asleep.

Chapter 5

Northern Ireland 1945

Crowds of people came and went to the terrace on Whiterock, bringing with them plates of food and kind words.

"It's bad enough when our children die fighting for Ireland and freedom, but fighting for the cause of the Brits . . ." Mary Helen heard coming from some of those in attendance. She heard it all in a state of fog. It wasn't real, couldn't be real. It was someone else's brother that had died, not hers. Any minute now he would burst through that door, swirl her in a hug and laugh at everyone's surprise. He always loved a grand entrance. She wouldn't believe it till she saw it.

The body was being shipped home but she wasn't allowed to see it.

"We've cleaned him up as best as we could, but it's still not pretty."

"I have to see him. I have to see my Jimmy," her mother had insisted. She took one look to confirm that it was her son then broke down in tears. Her father stepped forward, took a look and said, "That's him." He put his arm around his wife to guide her out when she straightened her shoulders and stated, "We'll be moving him to our home for a proper wake and burial."

"But, the body has already started to decompose."

"We'll be moving the casket. My boy deserves a proper wake," she insisted.

Liam was able to get home for the wake and funeral before returning to his company.

"He was the best of us," Liam stated at the wake, taking a shot of whiskey off of the casket and downing it. Mary Helen had never been close to Liam, but even she didn't recognize her brother. He had been changed in ways she didn't understand.

Mary Helen had been surprised when, only two weeks after the funeral, she came home to find her father preparing to host guests, three young American soldiers. Her granny had been furious and refused to come down to dinner.

"What are you doing, having Yanks over for dinner and your son not even cold in the grave?" she had questioned.

"I was at D-Day when the sea turned red with the blood of Americans. They are not the enemy. They fought alongside the Irish. This is my way to pay them back."

Granny spat on the ground. "This is what I think of any soldiers but IRA. Your father would be turning in his grave." She made the sign of the cross as she always did whenever she mentioned her deceased husband.

"Well, Da isn't here to argue with you and I'm not about to start. This is my home and I invite whomever I please."

Mary Helen suspected her mother was none too pleased either, but this was one of those rare occasions when she let him have his way. These were soldiers he had met at his job at the hotel. They had chatted and mentioned how much they missed home cooking so he had invited them.

"Mary Helen, set the table," he instructed her. "Then go upstairs and make yourself presentable for our guests. You, too, woman," he told his wife.

The conversation was subdued. Mary Helen's mother was too lost in her grief to want to talk to anyone who had been involved in the war. Mary Helen felt uncharacteristically uncomfortable sitting at the table with the Yanks. She caught one of them staring at her, then lowered her eyes to the plate of food in front of her. That left her dad, grandfather and Brigid to carry on the conversation.

"We're very sorry to hear about the loss of your son, Ma'am," one of the soldiers addressed Mary Helen's mother. "We've lost many a good friend in battle. We were proud to fight alongside the Irish." Martha didn't respond.

"Aye, well, that is war," her da responded for his wife. "There's hardly a family that hasn't lost someone in this war or previous wars."

"Not to mention the fighting between the Catholics and the Prods. Are you Catholic?" Granda Mike asked, staring them down. The soldiers glanced at each, unsure how to respond.

"How much longer will you be stationed in Belfast?" Brigid changed the subject.

"Don't know. There's still fighting in the Pacific. We could be ordered there at any time. Though I hope we get to stay here for a while yet." He smiled at Brigid.

"I would like to get some Japs, but Ireland is not without its attraction." The Yank who had been caught staring at Mary Helen looked in her direction again, then back to Brigid when Mary Helen didn't look up.

Mary Helen was relieved to have an excuse to leave the table as she and Brigid cleared the dishes, leaving the men to talk of war. She was surprised to find out after they had gone that arrangements had been made for her and Brigid to show the men the town on Saturday.

"That will be swell," one of the group smiled at Brigid, "See you, Saturday."

"Some of us have work to do," Mary Helen muttered after they left. "It would have been nice to have a say in the matter."

"The least you could have done was be more civilized," Brigid complained.

"Jimmy not even cold in the grave and all you're thinking about is going out, and with Americans at that."

"There's nothing wrong with Americans. We have a lot of family in the states," her da added.

"Well, I'll go, but I won't promise to be civilized," Mary Helen agreed.

That Saturday afternoon passed by pleasantly. Mary Helen had finally been formally introduced to the young man who had been staring at her during dinner. The introductions then had been perfunctory.

"My name is PFC Howard Jones. Pleased to meet you." Howard smiled and extended his hand to her as they followed along behind Brigid and the two other soldiers.

"Howard Jones, that's quite an American name."

"Is it? How so?"

"Jones, how can you get more American than that? So non-descript, so general. It doesn't speak to me of any nationality. So appropriate for America, the great melting pot. You might as well be Howard Nobody. Isn't every other American named either Smith or Jones?"

"Not quite, but quite a few. And what about you?"

"I'm Mary Helen Maguire. Pleased to meet you." Mary Helen nodded her head curtly and continued walking.

"Well, how can you get more Irish than that, Mary Maguire? The only name you're missing is Kathleen."

"Mary Helen," she corrected him. "And my confirmation name is Kathleen."

"There you have it, Mary Helen Kathleen. Me, a purebred American, which actually is a mutt since, as you stated, America is the great melting pot. With a purebred Irish colleen. 'Tis a marriage made in heaven," he jumped in front and faced her, trying to tease a smile out of her.

Mary Helen resisted the urge to smile. "And what reason would I have to smile, my brother being dead?"

"You are so much prettier when you smile, Mary Helen Kathleen." Howard continued, unwilling to allow her to remain sad.

"Are you saying I'm not pretty when I'm not smiling?"

"No, not at all. You are beautiful regardless, but your face is radiant when you smile. Mary Helen, just like the day I first saw you, when you were dancing on the green."

"You saw me then?"

"Yes, and I asked, who is that beguiling young woman with the stars radiating from her eyes?"

"Mr. Jones, I believe that would be what we Irish call blarney."

"It's only blarney when it's not true." He tentatively reached for her hand and smiled when she didn't pull it away, both looking straight ahead as they walked holding hands, smiling. It had been a pleasant afternoon, followed by many more such afternoons.

The summer passed with dates and pleasantries. It was a welcome and necessary diversion from her grief over her brother's death. That summer in Belfast had been quiet. Even the Orange celebration on July 12 couldn't detract for long from Mary Helen's happiness.

"What is all of that about?" Howard had asked when he saw a parade with men wearing orange sashes and carrying British flags. Mary Helen pulled him away from the street.

"We'll have none of that," she said as they walked away from the parade.

"Why?"

"It's the Orange men, celebrating the victory of the protestant King Billy of Orange over good King James. Even in quiet times, there's likely to be fighting." Howard looked back, wanting to see more, but gave in to Mary Helen. She was reluctant to talk about problems between the Catholics and Protestants.

Brigid did not receive the marriage proposal from the young American that she had hoped for, so quickly turned to the returning Irish soldiers in hope of a prospect for marriage.

Mary Helen, however, received a proposal and a promise from her young American, the promise to either come back for her or send for her.

"I know you are too young right now, but as soon as I'm able, I'll send for you. Once you're of marrying age, that is. Will you wait for me?" Mary Helen had given him no such promise.

"How can I know me own mind when I've never been anywhere, done anything. I'm not ready to promise yet."

"Then I'll promise you. I'll wait for you to be ready." And so they had left it at that. Her parents knew about the relationship but didn't push her in either direction.

"Best to be letting her make up her own mind," her father said. He had been keen on getting Brigid married, but wasn't ready yet to let his youngest daughter fly away from home. She returned to her position in the shirt factory with the title, almost engaged, plastered on her forehead in her mind. Most Catholic youth at that time left school at fifteen, especially if they were able to find work. Mary Helen had been happy to join her sister Brigid at the shirt factory.

When her brother, Liam, was discharged, he came home for a little over a week, then was gone again. Mary Helen had worried about him, being out late at night, the company he kept.

"Never again will I kill for the British," he swore. "If I'm to kill or be killed, let it be in the fight for freedom," he had told his parents when he left to join the IRA.

Chapter 6

Howard met Chloe's bus.

"Is that all you have?" he asked as he picked up the lone suitcase and rolled it away from the bus station.

"That's all."

"You travel light."

"I have a roommate. I left her all of the furniture. Another friend is taking my place while I'm gone. I've shipped the remainder of my clothes. It should arrive in a day or two."

So this is going to be for more than a day, Howard thought to himself as he approached the car.

"Here, Grandpa, let me do that." Chloe picked up her suitcase and placed it in the trunk of his car.

"I could have done that."

"I know, but let me. I'm pregnant, not an invalid." Howard was relieved. At eighty-nine he didn't have the strength he once had. Still he didn't want to appear weak.

He remembered picking up his wife at the train station so many years ago. She had only had one bag, too. He had picked it up and picked her up as he hugged her. That had been so long ago. Now their granddaughter was here with their great-grandchild waiting to be born. He wished Helen were here to see her.

"Are you hungry?"

"I had a sandwich on the bus."

"Hardly enough to sustain one person for such a long trip, much less two."

"I am eating for two now," Chloe agreed with a smile.

"What will it be? Pizza or burgers?" He pulled into the local Wendy's and picked up a value meal on the way home. He smiled as he watched her eat her cheeseburger, then dip her fries into her Frosty.

"Your dad used to do that, too."

"Must be where I got it from. You sure you're not hungry, Grandpa?"

"I'll fix some soup if I get hungry later."

"You know, I don't expect you to wait on me. I can fix meals, help around the house. And I'm going to get a job to help out."

"Don't you worry about that. For now, let's get you settled." He showed her into the spare bedroom and gave her towels then left her to unpack.

It felt strange, having another person in the house. He wasn't sure about it, but he thought it would be okay, at least for a while.

"What do you think?" he asked his wife as was still his custom when he was alone.

"What do you mean? She's family. Our granddaughter. Of course she's welcome." Howard knew Helen would have insisted on her staying. That's how she had always been about family. She had grown up in a home with extended family. It didn't matter whether there was room or not. If they were family, they made room. She had had a hard time understanding his desire for space, their own space to be alone together once they were married. She hadn't understood his desire to have a home of their own before they got married.

"You don't love me. You are having second thoughts about getting married," she had said when he told her his plans to save for a home.

"No, I haven't changed my mind. I just want everything to be right when you come."

"It's you that I want. Isn't that enough?" It should have been enough, he told himself now. Now he had a house and all he wanted was her.

Back then they did not have the ability to make oversees phone calls on a regular basis. Their conversations had been relegated to mail. Was there any wonder that miscommunications and misunderstandings had occurred? And when they did occur, he couldn't pick up a phone and call or hop on a jet to Northern Ireland. Was it any wonder that there were problems? The wonder was that despite the miles, despite the difficulties, they had eventually ended up together. And now, those letters were precious keepsakes.

Chloe came into the room, her hair wrapped in a towel, with sweat pants on and a large sweat shirt covering her growing belly.

"Did you find everything you need?" he asked.

"Yes, thanks, Grandpa." She sat down to watch TV with him, tucking her feet underneath her on the couch.

"You know, you have to tell your parents sometime."

"I know, Grandpa. I will. I just wish I knew what I was going to do."

"What are you talking about?"

"Whether I will keep the baby or not."

"What about the father?"

"He's okay with whatever I decide."

"Oh." Howard sat silent, staring at the TV.

"Yes." Howard could tell his granddaughter was waiting for him to say more. When he didn't she added. "I think he might be relieved." Again she waited before talking. "I'm not asking for child support."

"Why not?" Howard finally spoke.

"Because it was my decision to have the baby in the first place."

"I think he had something to do with it."

"Yes, but not the decision to have the baby. It's not fair for me to expect him to be saddled with a baby for the rest of his life just because I wasn't willing to have an abortion." Chloe avoided her grandfather's look as she mentioned the possibility of an abortion. "And it's not fair to expect him to pay if I don't give the baby up for adoption. I'll take care of my baby myself."

"Maybe he would want to know he has a child. Maybe he would like to be involved."

"No, it would put a cramp on his career. It's cramping my career. I haven't given up my apartment, just sublet it. I can give the baby up for adoption and return to my life in New York."

"Is that what you want?"

"I don't know what I want. All I know is that I'm having this baby. I'll figure out the rest later."

"You have to tell your parents some time."

"Yeah, but not yet. You won't tell my parents, will you?" Chloe looked him full in the face. "Please."

Howard shook his head no, but said, "Okay."

"Thank you, Grandpa. I knew I could count on you," she gave him a kiss on his cheek before going to bed.

Chapter 7

Northern Ireland – Autumn 1945

"Mary Helen," a voice called her name as she and her friends were walking home from one of the many dances they attended. She may be almost engaged, but she was still young and loved to dance. She didn't see any reason to stay home so she dressed in high heels and nylons, as befitting her new status as an almost betrothed young woman. Mary Helen and Brigid were both accomplished seamstresses from their job in the shirt factory so they had the best of gear to go out in. Mary Helen loved any form of dancing, including traditional Irish dance and ballroom dance. She had taken dance lessons along with all of her friends. After all, you couldn't get a boyfriend if you didn't know how to dance.

"Aye." Mary Helen recognized the voice. It was one of her brother Jimmy's friends, Owen Sullivan, one from whom Jimmy had defended her.

"I'm the only one who gets to tease my sister," Jimmy had said as he landed a fist in Owen's face.

"Can you get a message to your brother Liam?" Owen asked.

"You best be the one doing that. He's left home, went off with the IRA."

"Shhhh, best not to be blabbing that, lassie. Give this to Brigid then. She'll be able to get it to him." He placed the note in her hand and slipped away into the shadows.

"What does he mean, give it to Brigid?" Mary Helen wondered as she walked home. Brigid had been acting strange lately, but not too strange. Her sister had always been a question mark to her. One minute all goodness and light, and then surprising her with a streak of rebellion. Many days she did not know who her sister was. She, herself, was consistently rebellious, resisting the chores assigned her as a girl, resisting the stereotypes of what a girl was supposed to do or be. But Brigid, no such thing. Brigid was daddy's girl, doing whatever her da wanted, while Mary Helen was more inclined to be like her mother, a fire brand fighting her father at every turn and loving him for it. That was the one thing missing in her relationship with Howard.

It was so easy. He was easy to get along with. There was none of the fire of her parents' relationship, but then, at times it seemed her parents fought so much that they couldn't be friends. She didn't want this in a relationship. That was all the more reason to love Howard, that their relationship wasn't like her parents, she told herself. And besides, he gave her chocolate and nylon stockings. What was there not to like?

Aye, Brigid had been acting unlike herself lately, sneaking out when she thought no one knew. Mary Helen knew. She couldn't help but know, sharing the same bed in the same bedroom. She noticed Brigid slipping into bed at the wee hours of the morning.

"Where have you been?" she asked her sister.

"Never you mind. Go back to sleep. It's none of your business."

And now that note for Liam. She had thought Brigid had a secret beau. Could she be mixed up in IRA business?

Mary Helen confronted Brigid after the dinner dishes had been cleaned and put away.

"Owen Sullivan gave me this to give to you to give to Liam." She handed the note to Brigid. "What are you up to? Do you know where Liam is?" Brigid read the note then shook her head.

"Aye, but you best not be getting involved in this."

"And what is it that I best not be doing?" Mary Helen was not going to be pushed aside so easily. Brigid looked about the empty kitchen then took Mary Helen outside.

"We don't want Mum and Da to hear."

"They know he's involved with the IRA." Many respectable Catholic men and women were involved with the IRA. There was no reason to be concerned about that.

"Aye, but they don't know what he is doing, and it is best it stay that way. It's also best that you don't know."

"Brigid, you tell me right now, or I'll tell Mum and Da about you being gone at night."

Brigid paused to think, looked about in the darkness, then pulled her sister close. "Okay, it's IRA business but that's all I can tell you." Mary Helen suspected as much.

"And what about you?"

"I've just attended some of their meetings. Nothing more."

"But if Mum and Da find out . . ."

"They won't find out, right? Not from you anyway."

Mary Helen looked at her sister with new-found admiration. She would never have thought her capable of this, deceiving her mum and da, sneaking out at night. The IRA was something but . . .

"Only if you take me with you. Just one time."

"Are you crazy? You aren't even eighteen."

"But I'm almost engaged. That puts me ahead of you." That had been a low blow, Mary Helen realized, but it worked as Brigid agreed.

"Okay. Just be silent and don't cause any trouble. There's a meeting tomorrow night at nine. You can say you are babysitting."

"How did you find out about this?"

"Brian O'Connor, he invited me."

"Sean O'Connor's brother?"

"Aye, now be quiet about this." Mary Helen remembered Sean O'Connor. He had been in Jimmy's grade in school. He had always been nice to her. When the rest of Jimmy's friends had picked on her, he had been nice. She had had a crush on him back then. She wondered what he was up to, looked forward to seeing him.

The meeting was held in a room in the back of O'Shea's bar. The room was full of young men, only a few women besides herself and Brigid. Brigid pointed out one of the men in the front.

"There's Sean. He just got out of prison." Mary Helen looked in the direction Brigid had indicated. There in the front of the room was himself, Sean O'Connor, just as she remembered him only more rugged, more handsome. She remembered him as a skinny tall boy with dark brown hair. Now he was a skinny man though his arms showed muscles which hinted at more such muscles on his chest, hidden by his shirt. He was skinny but not a weakling. Of that she was sure. His face was darker, showing a shadow of whiskers, and his expression was serious as he listened to the first men speak. She remembered he had always seemed to be a serious young man, but there had been kindness in his smile when he had talked to her. At the end of the meeting, he stood up and thanked everyone for coming.

"C'mon, Sean will be getting this message to Liam," Brigid led her through the crowd to the group around the O'Connor brothers.

"Brian, Sean, I've got a message for Liam." Brigid handed them the note. Sean looked at Mary Helen.

"And who might this be?" he asked.

"My sister," Brigid started.

"Little Mary Helen," Sean said with the smile Mary Helen remembered from her childhood.

"Not so little anymore," Mary Helen replied. It was important to her that he realize she was no longer the little girl she once was.

"It's sorry I am about your brother. He was a good man, and a good friend. Better friend than many."

"And a good brother," Mary Helen stated. Sean nodded his head in agreement.

"What brought you to our meeting?"

"The note from Liam."

"I'll see that he gets it. It was good to see you, Mary Helen Maguire." He smiled before turning back to his conversation with the men gathered.

"Good to see you, too." She longed to say something more, but couldn't think what as Brigid led her away.

Chapter 8

Northern Ireland - 1945

Without Howard to distract her from her grief, Mary Helen found herself sinking inside herself. She was no longer the light-hearted, fun-loving girl she had been. She attributed this to the fact that she was almost engaged and thus had to behave in a manner befitting someone who was almost engaged. Any thought of Jimmy was quickly dismissed.

Her mother was not like herself either. It seemed all the fight had gone out of her, leaving her but a shell. She went to work each day, took care of the house, and stared at times into the darkness. Much as Mary Helen did not want to emulate her parents' marriage, she missed the fighting that had been their marriage. Her father drank, as was his custom, but it seemed without his wife nagging and screaming at him about his drinking, all of the fun had gone out of it. He sat home and drank, avoiding his friends at the pub.

Mary Helen became more helpful around the house, no longer looking for ways to get out of every chore, but willingly taking on new chores to help her mother and grandmother. She got up early to help her grandmother with the fireplace.

"Granny, what is it you are saying when you stoke the flames?" Mary Helen could see her grandmother's lips moving and hear a whisper as she blew on the coals left over from the previous night's fire and coaxed it back into life. The smell of ash filled her nostrils as she watched.

"It's a blessing prayer to start a new day. There are many blessing prayers."

"Would you teach me, Granny?"

"Perhaps someday we'll have gas heat and you won't have to fret about that fire anymore." Mary Helen's father came into the room.

"It's our heritage. We mustn't forget the old ways. A blessing for everything," his mother corrected him.

"A lot of good your blessing did for my Jimmy, old woman." Mary Helen's mother joined the gathering. It was the first bit of life she had seen in her mother since Jimmy's passing.

"Blessings aren't magic. They don't protect from all harm or we Catholics wouldn't have graveyards full of young men cut down in their prime, or whole families lost during the potato famine. Still they are reminding us of God's presence amidst suffering," Granny said.

"Don't talk about God, old woman. Where was your God when my son died fighting a war that wasn't his own? Where was your God during the famine? If there is a God, I'm thinking he is more absent than present."

"Sacrilege." Granny made a sign of the cross.

"Curses on your religion. It's religion that's causing all the problems in Ireland, Catholics and Prods are both to blame. I'll have none of either of them."

Granny crossed herself again and mouthed prayers under her breath. Mary Helen didn't know what to think. Her mother had never spoken against the Church before. There had been hints of discord over the years, yet she faithfully attended church every Sunday and required the same of her children.

"It'll be to the priest you'll go to confess your blasphemy," Granny said.

"I'm confessing to no priest. If God was a forgiving God, he would never have taken my Jimmy away." Mary Helen didn't know what to do. At least her mother was fighting again. This was better than the sullen sad woman who had been inhabiting her mother's body, but she wasn't sure about the woman who had come to take her place.

Her father tried to intervene between the two women only to be pushed aside by both.

"I'll none of you or your Church. For now, God is dead to me like my child. I'll be on my way." With that she exited the kitchen and proceeded down the street. Mary Helen ran after her.

"But Mum, you haven't had any breakfast. And what about lunch?"

"I've no need for breakfast or lunch. I've work to do." Martha paused, looked at her daughter then kissed her on her forehead. "Now go you on back to home, get ready for work. It's afterwards I'll see you."

Mary Helen wasn't sure what to make of this new situation. After declaring her freedom from religion, her mother never returned to church. She insisted that the rest of the family attend as they had in the past, while she stayed home alone to nurse her grief. When the priest came to check in on his lost sheep, she threw him out. The rest of the family had been waiting outside to give them privacy when the sound of yelling exploded and Fr. Dougherty came running outside followed by Martha with a frying pan. That was his last attempt to get her back into church.

Since seeing Sean O'Connor at that meeting, Mary Helen found she wasn't as interested as she had been in going to local dances. Again she attributed it to the fact that she was almost engaged, but that hadn't stopped her before.

Her focus became her housework, learning the ways of the past from Granny and Granda Mike. She was determined that when Howard came to get her, she would know how to set up an Irish household in an American town. She would bring a bit of Ireland with her to America.

"Granda?" she would sit next to him at night before he was too far in his cups. "Tell me about the old times."

"Are you wanting to hear about Finn McCool, the giant?"

"No, Granda, I'm not a child. It's about the Anglo-Irish War I'm wanting to know. Our history."

"There's not much to tell."

"Tell me how my Granda Tom died." Granny's husband had served in the IRA with Granda Mike. They had been together when he died.

"It is what it is," he responded. "It was a war, people were killed. Sure, what else could you do?"

"And you were in prison?"

"A smaller prison from the one I'd been living in."

"What do you mean, Granda?"

"Men without freedom, Ireland without a free country, might as well be living in a prison. Better to be inside a prison than live in a country without freedom." Try though she might, she couldn't get him to tell her more than that.

And then there was Sean O'Connor. Sean had gotten a job at the docks. Since their losses and the war with Germany, the IRA was back in the shadows. He needed something to do until ready to take up arms again.

"You again," he said, puffing his cigarette and smiling as she came outside after a dance. "I'm thinking you best be busy about woman's work."

"And that would be?"

"Taking care of the home and preserving the Irish way." That was precisely what Mary Helen had been doing but hearing it come out of his mouth made it feel like it was wrong.

"That's none of your business, what I'm doing with my time."

"What would your brother think, you wasting your life at dances?"

"Some brother he is. He shows up for one week then it's gone he is."

"That doesn't mean he doesn't care." Mary Helen could feel anger rising into her throat as he spoke. He put out his cigarette. "Really, you shouldn't be here. It might not be safe. I'll walk you home."

"I'm perfectly capable of walking myself home," Mary Helen asserted.

"I'm sure you are. Humor me, for the sake of your brother, Jimmy. It's what he would be wanting." At that Mary Helen had to relent.

"You know I'm almost engaged," she told him as they strolled along the road.

"Are you now?" Sean seemed to think this funny. "And to whom might that be?"

"No one you know. An American."

"Oh," Sean considered this. "An American GI, working his ways with our women through nylons and chocolate."

"It's nothing like that."

"It isn't. Then what is it?"

"He wants me to marry him."

"And where is that GI now? Back in America?"

"No, he's in the Pacific, in Japan. Once he has enough money he's going to send for me."

"Is he now," Sean said no more, implying everything.

"Yes, he is. Don't you go talking against him. You don't know him."

"No, but know you, I do, Mary Helen, and you deserve better than a GI who promises the world but doesn't deliver."

"He isn't like that."

"For your sake, I hope he's not." They arrived at her home. "I'll be leaving you here, Miss Mary Helen Maguire."

"That you will, Mr. Sean O'Connor." Mary Helen ran up the stairs into her home without looking back. But the seed of doubt had been planted. She pulled out the letters written from somewhere in Japan.

I had wanted to get some Japs after Pearl Harbor and what they had done to us, but now it is too late. We are here to "mop up" you might say, but what I've found wasn't what I expected. The hospitals are full of Japanese with radiation sickness, not to mention the thousands killed in Hiroshima and Nagasaki. They say it was necessary. If they hadn't done that the war may have gone on for years. Countless American lives would have been lost, including possibly mine. I guess I'm grateful for that, but so much suffering. War truly is hell.

I've only been on the sidelines. I don't want to think about what it must have been like for those in the middle of the conflict. There are other soldiers I've met here who were at Iwo Jima. Their stories of the blood . . . They survived, but did they? They wake up screaming from the memories.

I'm so grateful for the memories I have of you. When woken by their screams, I think of you. I remember you dancing when I first met you. The memory of our time together and your love sustain me through difficult times. I can't wait till we can be together forever.

Love,
Howard

Mary Helen clasped the letter to her chest, comforted by those words. He loves me. He will return for me.

Convinced of this, she fell asleep, wiping away the doubt inspired by Sean.

Chapter 9

"You know, she has a lot of potential," Patrick told Kathleen as he changed out of his dance shoes, packed them away and prepared to leave. Ashley was in the corner of the room practicing her dance steps. He stood up and nodded in Ashley's direction. "She could compete nationally. With all of her ballet training, she's a natural."

Kathleen watched Ashley kick, hands straight to her side. Her outstretched leg formed a right angle with her body with each kick, then landed gracefully on her toes.

"Of course she will never reach that potential with only one lesson a week, and that one a group lesson," Patrick added.

"Of course not." Kathleen raised her eyebrows, knowing where this was heading.

"I'm just saying, to reach her full potential she needs lessons at least twice a week, maybe some private lessons, too."

"And how much would that cost?"

"She could join my intermediate group. It's the same price as this class. However she would have to come to Plymouth for the lesson."

"And the private lessons?"

"Well, maybe we can work something out."

"I'm sure we can." Kathleen cocked her head to the side as she thought.

"Work out what?" Dale asked as he approached the two.

"More dance lessons for Ashley," Kathleen explained.

"More? She already spends every afternoon after school here. How much more time can she spend in dance lessons?"

"She could win at Nationals, maybe even go on to the World Championship." Patrick added.

"What are you talking about?" Howard joined the conversation.

"Ashley going to the International competition in Irish dancing," Kathleen explained.

"My granddaughter did that, years ago while she was in high school," Howard said.

"The one who's staying with you now?" Kathleen asked. "You never told us that."

"There's lots I haven't told you."

"Really, because I thought I had heard all of your stories."

"I've hardly gotten started," Howard smiled.

"Maybe your granddaughter could teach Ashley, save the drive to Plymouth," Kathleen suggested.

"Not just anyone can teach Irish step dancing," Patrick objected.

"What are you talking about?" Ashley made her presence known, her hands on her hips and her eyes flashing as she pursed her lips and stared them down. "I don't like being talked about behind my back."

Kathleen remembered Joy, Ashley's mother complaining about people whispering about her. "I hate it when you talk like I'm not in the room," she had said with her eyes closed. It was obvious where Ashley got her spunk.

"We were just talking about how good you've gotten," Dale attempted to placate her.

"We were talking about you taking additional dance classes," Patrick explained. "Would you like to compete in the feis coming up?" A feis was traditionally a Gaelic festival but had come to be associated with dance competitions.

Ashley's forehead crinkled as she considered the possibility. Kathleen wondered what was going on in that head. Ashley had enjoyed going to the competition last year. She had competed in the beginner's section and placed even though she had only been taking lessons for five months. "Would I have to have one of those dresses like the other girls?"

"Not yet. As an advanced beginner, you could compete in a white blouse and black skirt, like last summer, or you could wear the school uniform." The uniform was a red dress with white embroidery but not as flashy as what Kathleen had seen other girls wear.

"Then okay. That would be fun."

"How much is this going to cost me?" Dale whispered to Kathleen. Kathleen was well aware of his financial situation from handling Joy's bills the last years of her life. Dale wasn't broke, but he was still paying off his wife's hospital bills.

"Don't worry. I'll work something out," Kathleen assured him then spoke to Ashley and Patrick, "We'll talk about it, see what we can work out." As the director of the dance studio, Kathleen was prepared to intervene on the part of her niece and brother.

"You're forgetting my granddaughter," Howard asserted.

"What about your granddaughter?" Kathleen asked.

"Maybe she could teach Ashley. She's a dancer from New York. I thought maybe she could help out. Chloe, come over here," Howard called to the young woman waiting outside the classroom. There was no fat on her dancer's body. The small bulge of a baby was apparent under her loose clothes. She paused and looked at her grandfather before approaching.

"Come join us," Howard repeated the invitation. The extra weight wasn't affecting the grace of her stride as she approached and extended a hand in welcome. Kathleen took her hand, quickly sizing her up.

"Come on, Ashley, you've got homework to do," Dale said as he escorted his daughter out of the room.

"So, you've done Irish step dancing before," Patrick inquired. He asked about her training. "Why did you stop?"

"I had other interests. Competing internationally was pretty much consuming all of my time. I wanted to be a regular teenager for a while, and then I set my sights on Broadway. Irish step dancing wasn't going to get me a part on Broadway," Chloe explained.

"So, show me what you got," Patrick put her through a number of steps. Her additional weight didn't slow her down any. Kathleen watched, remembering how Joy had continued to dance into the last months of her pregnancy with Grace.

"She know other dance styles?" Kathleen asked Howard.

"You name it. A little bit of everything, ballet, tap, jazz."

Patrick appeared impressed despite himself. "She could be a suitable coach for Ashley and with some more training might make an okay teacher. Mind you though, she needs more training. It's one thing to dance, another to teach."

"And you would teach her?" Kathleen asked.

"When she brings Ashley to Plymouth for her lessons," he agreed with a smile, closing the deal.

Chapter 10

"So, how did it go?" Howard asked as they drove home.

"Good. I'm going to assist in some of the classes. It's not a lot of money, but it's a start."

"Well, they are already fully staffed. Next year, after the baby is born, you'll be able to get your own classes to teach."

"Who says I'll still be here next year?"

Howard didn't answer. He picked up a pizza on the way home for dinner. "To celebrate your new job," he told her. Chloe smiled in response.

"Grandpa?" Chloe said over the pizza.

"Yes."

"I thought Grandma's name was Helen."

"It was."

"But on your marriage certificate it says Mary Helen."

"Have you been snooping?" Howard put down his pizza and looked up at her.

"No, just looking. It is hanging in my bedroom." Chloe shrugged her shoulders and lowered her eyes to her pizza.

"Her full name was Mary Helen, but she went by Helen."

"And I thought you met Grandma when you were in Ireland after World War II?" Chloe continued to focus on the pizza, pulling a string of cheese off and lowering it into her mouth.

"Yes, I did." Howard continued to look at Chloe as she played with her food.

"But you didn't get married until 1952. That's seven years later. Why? What happened?"

"So many questions," Howard paused. "That's a long story."

"I have plenty of time. Tell me." Chloe finished off the cheese on her fingers and looked directly at Howard.

Howard breathed in as he gathered his thoughts. How much to tell her? How much did she need to know? How much did he want her to know? He had never told her dad this story.

"We met after the war, but she was only sixteen at the time. Too young to get married."

"So why didn't you marry when she turned eighteen?"

"It's more complicated than that. I couldn't just leave the army."

"Other people in the army got married."

Howard shifted in his seat. He wasn't comfortable with this questioning. It was like having to answer to Helen again. Howard remembered those years in Japan when shipped out of Ireland. How he had tossed and turned.

"It wasn't that easy. I went from Ireland to Japan. I had missed out on the war in Europe, and I missed out on the fighting in Japan. I felt like a phony. I rode in after others had done the hard work and yet I received accolades, at least that had been the case in Ireland. In Japan there were no accolades. There we were an occupying army, hated by those occupied. But the U.S. government was committed to helping the Japanese get back on their feet after the devastation of the two Atomic bombs. I hadn't wanted to be there, but I had no choice.

"Once the war was over, I figured there was no reason for me to remain in the Army, except the papers I had signed when I enlisted said something else. I had to complete my tour of duty. When I had signed up, I hadn't thought about the years of life I was signing away, hadn't thought about anything but getting the Japs. Once I was there, I was seeing that they were just humans like anyone else. I had wanted to hang onto the image of them as monsters, lurking in the dark, taking American lives. On my days off I toured the city, toured the hospitals, even went to Nagasaki. I saw the destruction imposed on this people. I saw that they were men with families they cared for, wives and children, not the murderers I had imagined them to be.

"Once the war was over I wanted to go home, get on with my new life, but the Army had another idea. My term wouldn't be up for six months or more, so I was stuck. I decided to make the best of this time by finishing high school so I would be ready to start college when I was discharged.

"I had thought, maybe Mary Helen could join me. We could live in married housing while I attend college, I planned. But first I had to be discharged."

"So what happened?"

Howard got up and cleared the plates from the table. "That's enough for tonight."

Chapter 11

Northern Ireland - 1946

Mary Helen carefully blew on the coals in the fireplace as she prayed, the Gaelic from her childhood slipping over her tongue:

> *"I will kindle my fire this morning*
> *In the presence of the holy angels of heaven,*
> *In the presence of Ariel of the loveliest form,*
> *In the presence of Uriel of the myriad charms,*
> *Without malice, without jealousy, without envy,*
> *Without fear, without terror of any one under the sun,*
> *But the Holy Son of God to shield me.*
> *   Without malice, without jealousy, without envy,*
> *   Without fear, without terror of any one under the sun,*
> *   But the Holy Son of God to shield me."*

The first stanza was to invite angels into the home, with God at the center, Granny had told her. It was also a prayer of protection from dark forces: malice, jealousy, envy and fear. The second stanza spoke to the heart.

> *"God, kindle Thou in my heart within*
> *A flame of love to my neighbor,*
> *To my foe, to my friend, to my kindred all,*
> *To the brace, to the knave, to the thrall,*
> *O Son of the loveliest Mary,*
> *From the lowliest thing that liveth,*
> *To the Name that is highest of all."* *

Her grandmother had caught cold and a cough and was confined to bed. Mary Helen dutifully took on her chores, starting the fireplace against the winter chill that had settled into the terrace, thinking of her grandmother as she recited her prayers.

The ritual was soothing, taking her mind off of her troubles.

It was six months since the end of the war in the Pacific. She hoped each day for a letter from Howard saying he had been discharged and would be coming for her.

In his last letter Howard had explained about trouble at home. Certainly she knew about trouble at home. All of her life had been troubles. Now she was anxious to have a home of her own, but the money to go to the States had yet to appear.

My brothers are both home from the war too, only they were not as lucky as me. Howard had written in his last letter. *"George came home in a wheel chair and Ronald . . . well, Ronald is physically okay as far as we know, but mentally, he's not there. Shell shock. Mom needs me to help at home. Dad needs my help in the store. I'll be taking classes at night to get my degree and get a good job. Right now most of my money is needed to help my family but I'm setting aside every spare penny I've got."*

It had not been what Mary Helen wanted to hear. Why, she could work in the store. She could help in the house. She just needed to get there.

And then there was Sean O'Connor. He seemed to keep showing up at all of the clubs, wherever they went dancing.

"Heard anything more from your American GI?" he always asked.

"Aye, I have, though I'm thinking it's none of your business."

"If you were my girl, I wouldn't leave you alone starving after a letter or two."

"No, you'd be leaving me for your war."

"It's our war. We Catholics, we'll never be treated equally by the Brits or the Prods unless we stand up for ourselves."

"And use violence?"

"If necessary."

"The war is over. I'm thinking it's time to put an end to the fighting."

"Is that truly what you think? Because I'm thinking, no. I'm thinking you've got too much of your brothers in you to just sit by and allow the Brits to tell you what to do."

"Nobody tells me what to do."

"I can see that. Point proven," Sean smiled. Mary Helen wanted to slap the smile off of his face but resisted the impulse. That would just further prove his point. Instead she glared at him then started to walk away.

"Is that truly what you want?" Sean followed after her, still talking. "You just going to walk away when so many of us are crammed into small houses, not allowed to buy homes of our own. Waiting on lists for years for an opening only to be bumped by the first Protestant to apply. Is that how you want to live?"

Mary Helen didn't respond. She was well aware of the inequities. She knew the laws had been written by Protestants to protect their privileges and keep down the Catholic. Votes were restricted to those who owned property thus a family with several children of voting age who were forced to live with their parents because they were refused houses themselves only had two votes. In some places votes were linked to property value so those with higher valued homes were given extra votes.

"And now you are planning on leaving the country like so many others."

"And are you blaming me? What is there for me here?"

"Your brother wouldn't abandon his people."

"Aye, well Jimmy's dead and Liam might as well be for all we see of him."

"He's working for his people, to protect Catholics and Catholic interests."

"And what of his family?" They approached the terrace on Whiterock.

"What nonsense are you talking, girl?" she could hear her Granny's voice from where she sat on the steps, smoking her pipe. A faint glow appeared from the pipe as the smell of tobacco swirled about her. "Who is that you are talking to?"

"Sean O'Connor," Sean introduced himself. "Just making sure your granddaughter arrives home safely."

"Hmmm," Granny strained to see him in the dark. "You can leave now. Be off with ya." Granny sent him away. Sean smiled, bowed and with a wave of his hand was gone.

"Don't you be wasting your time with those O'Connor boys. You've got a good man in America. No need for the likes of him, rabble rouser."

"But Granny, weren't you in the IRA?"

"That I was. Still am. But sometimes these young ones take it too far. They don't know what war is like. Now get to bed." Mary Helen was familiar with this sentiment. The local folks supported the IRA but only so far. One minute they were heroes, but if they took the violence too far, they became scoundrels. She recognized the contradiction. They were cheered as protectors of Catholic rights, provided with safe homes to meet in but the tide of public opinion shifted if their actions were deemed too violent, killing women and children.

Sean had refused to join the Brits in fighting the Germans.

"That's their war, not mine," he had insisted. Instead he had joined the IRA, fighting the British. Her brothers had chosen to fight on the side of the British in the war, but look where that had left them. One gone, the other alienated from country and family as Liam met with remnants of the IRA in other parts of Ireland and Northern Ireland. The IRA may have gone back in the shadows for a while, but they weren't gone. They were just waiting for another opportunity. The time after the end of the war was quiet, so Sean, like others, had found work on the docks, biding his time.

Mary Helen found herself enjoying his company as she walked home from dances.

"What was it like in prison?" she asked him on one of these walks.

"Now, you aren't really wanting to know, are you?" Sean hesitated to tell her the details.

"I wouldn't be asking if I didn't want to know."

"It wasn't pretty, that I can say." He paused and lit a cigarette. "When the warders refused to give us status as the political prisoners we were, we started a 'strip strike'."

"What was that?" Mary Helen reached for his cigarette and took a puff. Sean continued walking, not meeting her gaze as he spoke.

"Well, we decided not to do a hunger strike because it weakens participants too much, sometimes to the point where they were never the same, sometimes to the point of death. So we refused to wear the prison clothes. In retaliation, the warders took away everything else from our cells, our bedding, blankets, even our handkerchiefs. They also took what little reading material we had, except for religious books." He lit another cigarette, letting Mary Helen keep his first one.

"The cell was bare during the day. We had very little to eat, tea and bread for breakfast, a pint of soup for dinner, then tea and porridge and milk in the afternoon. Those were long days. You might hear a knock on the wall and try talking to your neighbor until ordered 'off the pipes'. It was cold even though it was summer, there being no heat to warm the stones. At night they brought us blankets. We jumped right to bed, covered up and went to sleep, before another day of the same started."

"How long did that last?"

"It was three months till the strike was called off on account of John Graham's swollen knee. We called it off so he could get treatment."

"Things were better then?"

"As much as they can be while in prison. But enough of that. Let's talk of happier things." Sean stopped, put his cigarette out, then began to walk again. Mary Helen was glad for the change of subjects, but she didn't forget what he had told her.

Chapter 12

"So, Grandpa, you haven't told me the rest."

"The rest of what?"

"Of why you didn't marry Grandma until 1952.

"There's not much to tell."

"So tell me." Howard didn't want to go back there but Chloe wouldn't let it go. She sat at the table refusing to move as she waited for more of his story.

"I told you about my brothers, George and Ronald."

"Not really. I'd heard about Uncle George. He died a number of years ago. But I never heard about Uncle Ronald."

"That's because he died shortly after the end of the war."

Chloe waited as Howard gathered his thoughts. It wasn't that he didn't remember. He remembered it too well, like it was yesterday. But it was one of those memories he tried to push out of his mind.

Ronald just wasn't right when he came back. Howard was busy helping out at his dad's grocery store. His dad had tried to get Ronald to help out too, but Ronald refused. Most days he stayed in his darkened bedroom, staring at the wall. At night he would go to the local bar and hang out with other veterans. If he heard loud noises, or a car backfiring, he would jump down and lay on the floor until one of the other veterans gently urged him back up.

"I tried to get him to get help, but he refused."

"Help for what, Grandpa?"

"The nightmares. I could hear him screaming every night. Seemed he would drink until he fell asleep then woke up screaming. Then he would just stare at the wall."

"Didn't he talk to anyone?"

"I tried to get him to talk, but it just wasn't done back then. He didn't want to have anything to do with a psychiatrist, insisted he wasn't crazy. I tried to get him help through the Veterans' Administration but they were overwhelmed with returning vets and just getting established back then."

"Didn't Uncle George stay at the VA hospital?"

"For a while, but not at first. We set up a bedroom for him downstairs and put in a ramp. Ma was determined to take care of him herself. But George was better off than Ronald. We just didn't realize it right away. We thought he would snap out of it eventually. I remember my dad yelling at him to snap out of it. Didn't work."

It had not been pleasant, those years after the war. The one saving grace had been the nurse assigned to help with George's care. She came twice a week to check on him. George had been reluctant and grumpy at first.

"So, you're here to take care of the cripple," he would grumble. But as she didn't put up with any nonsense and persisted, he started to look forward to her visits, as did Howard.

"The only bit of sunshine back then was Sheila, George's nurse. She insisted George sit out on the porch rather than stay inside. She encouraged him to keep up with his physical therapy to get stronger. She didn't let him feel sorry for himself."

"The only cripple I see here is in your head. You can sit inside feeling sorry for yourself or accept your situation and make the best of it. Either way I get paid. It's all the same to me, but I'd rather be around someone who actually cares about himself," Sheila said.

"You tell him," Ronald came out of his room at the sound of her voice.

"And who are you to talk? Two good legs and moping around like you're disabled." Sheila was not one to mince words. She had seen too many hard cases and had learned to steel herself against feeling sorry for any of them. Still there was compassion under her firmness.

"That was Aunt Sheila, right?"

"Yes, eventually, but not right away. I was sweet on Sheila for some time."

"You were? What about Grandma?"

"We all were sweet on Sheila. That's part of the story."

"Okay. Go on."

"Well, Ronald was just never right. I don't know what triggered it."

"Triggered what, Grandpa?" Howard couldn't hear the impatience in Chloe's voice as he rambled. He was too busy reliving that day. He remembered it all too well, as if it were yesterday. He and his dad had closed the store early at his mom's urgings.

"Something's wrong," she had said. "Get home right away."

Howard hadn't argued when his dad insisted they both leave.

"Something's wrong. Your mother needs both of us." They locked the doors and hurried home. His mother met them at the door.

"What's wrong, Mother?" his dad asked.

"Ronald, he has a gun."

"Where did he get it?"

"I don't know. I just know he has one."

"Where is he?" his dad talked as he walked.

"Inside. George is trying to talk sense to him, but I don't know."

"You stay out here." Howard's dad instructed his wife as they entered the house. They found Ronald in the kitchen with George. He was waving a gun, talking crazy.

"You don't know. You don't know what it was like. They are out there."

"Ronald, I know. I know what it was like. I was in the war, too. I lost friends, too." George tried to calm him down.

"Bodies, bodies, everywhere, falling on top of me. I can't get up."

"It's over, Ronald. You're safe."

"No, I'm not. I hear their screams. I can't stop them."

"Put the gun down, son." Their father slowly approached Ronald. Ronald pointed the gun at him.

"You don't know."

"I know I don't know, son. Put the gun down and tell me about it."

"Do you hear them? Can't you hear them? I hear their voices."

"I don't hear them, son. Give me the gun and we'll talk." Ronald put the gun on the table and their dad approached him and slowly put his hand on his shoulder. Ronald pulled back.

Sheila arrived in the door. Howard tried to stop her.

"Your mother called. Thought maybe I could help," she said.

"No, it's too dangerous." Howard tried to hold her back until their dad took the gun from the table.

"It's okay now, Howard. Let her come in." Ronald was standing with his back to them. Sheila approached and touched him gently on the shoulder.

"Ronald, it's Sheila. It's okay. You're safe." Slowly Ronald turned around and allowed Sheila to hug him. She led him out of the kitchen and into the living room. George stayed in the living room with him as she talked with Howard and their father in the kitchen.

"He needs to go to the hospital. He needs professional care."

"No," their mother joined them. She began to protest until their dad gave her a look that kept her quiet.

"What do we have to do?" Howard asked.

"I'll make the arrangements. For now, we need to keep him calm until I can get someone to transport him to the hospital. And put that gun away. Where did he get it?"

"I thought it was safely hidden," Hector said.

"You have to get rid of it. You can't keep it here."

"I'll keep it at the store," Hector assured her. Sheila made the arrangements and someone came from the Veterans' Administration to take Ronald. His mother had watched without saying a word as her middle child was carried off in a van.

"Don't worry, Verna," Sheila had assured her. "He'll be okay. They'll take care of him."

Howard had gone out on the back porch for a smoke after the excitement. Sheila joined him.

"Got any more of those?" she asked. Howard clumsily reached into his pocket for a cigarette and his lighter. He handed her a cigarette and lit it. She took a long draw and sighed.

"Tough day," Howard commented.

"Not much more than other days."

"You've seen this before?"

"Yes, and worse." Sheila took another draw from the cigarette. She wasn't inclined to talk.

"Thank you," Howard finally said.

"Just doing my job." Sheila dismissed his gratitude. Howard couldn't help but notice how her hair framed her face in a short bob and the line of her neck as she looked up and took another drag from the cigarette. He turned away from her.

"It must be hard, all of those injured soldiers," he commented.

"You want to go to a movie?" Sheila faced him.

"What?"

"How about a movie?"

"Sure," Howard agreed. And so had started a pattern. Going to the movies was how Sheila escaped the hardships of her job. Howard was a willing companion in her escapes.

"I know you've got a fiancé in Ireland," Sheila had said after the first movie as he walked her home. Howard didn't respond. "George told me."

"Is that a problem?"

"Not for me. It's just a movie. Besides, you're too young for me." Sheila, at twenty-five, was well aware of the age difference. "So tell me about her." Sheila had known about Helen, but Helen hadn't known about Sheila, at least not until much later. Some things are better not mentioned in letters.

"But what about Grandma?" Chloe broke into his reverie.

"That's enough for tonight. More tomorrow." Howard didn't want to continue. He felt unfaithful to Helen just talking about this.

Chapter 13

Joy's Center for Healing and the Arts was doing better this year, making in-roads to be self-supporting, but there was still a ways to go. Thanks to businesses renting space, additional classes in the dance studio and some grant money, they were close to being out of debt, including paying Kathleen for the time she worked without being paid and paying Esther the money she had loaned them. Kathleen and Esther were both still working more hours than they were being paid for, but Kathleen hoped to have this remedied in a year or two. If all went according to plans, she would be paid for the full-time work she was putting in and even be able to give Letty a raise.

Letty had proven invaluable these last few years, first helping out when Joy was sick, then taking over the dance part of the studio and this past year, adding classes in modern dance and jazz. Now, with Chloe, they might be able to add two classes in Irish step dance, under the aegis of Patrick's school, but it would be less expensive than having Patrick travel to teach the classes. With Patrick it had been more a break-even proposition, with the studio benefitting from getting more people into the building but not making any money. If Chloe taught the classes they would have to pay something to Patrick but after Chloe's salary the studio would make a profit.

Yes, things were looking up for the center and the studio. Joy's legacy was secure. Joy had founded the dance studio years ago and eventually bought the building it was located in. She had been Kathleen's brother's wife, mother to Ashley, Jacob and Grace. When she died from cancer over two years ago, she had left the building, with all of the problems that entailed, to Kathleen. With the help of Esther, her mother, and other family and supporters, they had managed to not only keep the building open, but were on their way to securing Joy's legacy. It had not been what Kathleen had seen herself doing with her life, but perhaps it was what she needed to give her life purpose.

The dance studio still ran independently, under Kathleen's ownership and Letty's leadership. Joy's Center for Healing and the Arts had a board of directors overseeing its operation with Kathleen as the executive director. Pastor Joe was a board member, along with

Kathleen's new stepfather, Peter, and her brother's new girlfriend, Ava. It definitely was a family affair, even if a non-profit business. Pastor Joe was her mother's and her brother's pastor. Kathleen had gotten to know him during Joy's illness. His wife had died in a car accident eight years ago. He was now raising two teenage daughters, Stephanie and Michelle. Stephanie was the same age as Kathleen's youngest son, Scott. Both were seniors in high school. Kathleen had only started dating Pastor Joe the previous summer. Despite the break-up, she couldn't avoid him because of his position on the board and because his daughter, Michelle, was taking Irish dance lessons at the studio. They had both determined to be cordial to each other, saying hi when Joe came to pick Michelle up and exchanging polite conversation before and after board meetings.

Kathleen figured it had just been all the tension and stress of the previous years, dealing with Joy's cancer and death, being thrown together, that had brought them together. That wasn't enough to sustain a relationship. She didn't want to be living from one crisis to the next. Once the crises were over, it seemed they had little in common. He was a church pastor, she, an ex-con with no connections to church and no desire for one.

Yes, she had had some spiritual experiences the past few years. Joe had been instrumental in some of it, but that wasn't enough to get her in church. She and God were on good terms now. God wasn't demanding that she go to church, so she didn't see the need for it.

"I'm an okay person, aren't I" she had asked her mom when Esther tried to talk her into attending church with her.

"Yes, you are now." Kathleen realized Esther had gone through a lot with her in the past.

"See, I'm doing just fine without church."

"It's not that. There's more to church than that." Esther let it go. Kathleen was glad for that. Wasn't it enough that she finally had her life on track after so many years on a destructive path? Kathleen knew her mother had been disappointed when she broke up with Joe. She appreciated her mother staying out of it.

"You knew it was coming, Mom, didn't you? We are way too different."

"But sometimes opposites attract," Peter had interjected. Kathleen had grown to like him and accepted him into the family. Still he could be annoying at times.

"And sometimes they crash and burn. After the initial attraction, there has to be something more," Kathleen told him.

"Your mom broke up with my dad," Stephanie told Scott when she found out.

"No way."

"Yes. Dad didn't want to talk about it, but I finally got it out of him. I think it had something to do with Grandma and Grandpa coming for Christmas."

"I wondered why Mom didn't go over to your house on Christmas. She said your dad wanted time alone with your grandparents."

"No way. The last thing Dad wanted was to spend Christmas with Grandma and Grandpa. I think he wanted your mom around as a buffer between him and his parents. As it was, it was awkward what with Grandma and Grandpa asking about the woman he was dating and why couldn't they meet her. He didn't want to talk about it."

"This won't affect our friendship, will it?"

"Of course not. We were friends long before our parents started dating." Stephanie and Scott had been instrumental in bringing them together.

"That's good. At least now I know why Mom has been even more focused on her work than before."

"My dad, too. He's burying himself in work. Maybe we can get them back together."

"Not if it's going to end up with them fighting and breaking up again. I think it's best to forget about it," Scott insisted. Stephanie wasn't as ready to let it go.

Chapter 14

"You still haven't told me about Ronald. What happened?" This was becoming their dinner ritual. Chloe asking, Howard responding.

Howard looked down at his plate before beginning, picking at the macaroni and cheese with hot dogs cut up in it that Chloe had thrown together.

"Ronald appeared better when he came home from the hospital. He even started to help out at the store. I began to think I might be able to go to school full-time instead of just nights since he was helping Dad out. However it was just a ruse to get access to Dad's gun again. We received another frantic call from Mom several months after his discharge. We don't know what caused the break. He seemed to be doing so good. He had started spending time with Sheila. It seemed to be going well, then . . ." The cheese on his plate was congealing as he pushed around the macaroni.

"What happened, Grandpa?"

"I don't know if he broke up with Sheila or she broke up with him or it just wasn't going anywhere. Never did find out. We got home and he was in the kitchen again with the gun." Howard found himself once more back in another time and another place. He remembered rushing home with his dad.

"You'd be better off without me. Everyone would be better off without me," they heard Ronald saying as they walked in the front door. They could hear Verna and George's voices assuring Ronald that that wasn't true. George calmly told Ronald to put the gun down as Ronald paced about the kitchen. When Howard and his dad came into the kitchen, Ronald shouted, "Who called them? I told you not to call them."

"It's okay, son," Hector quietly approached him. "Put the gun down."

"I'm not going back to that hospital."

"Just put the gun down. We won't send you back. Just put the gun down," Hector insisted.

"You don't understand. No one understands." Ronald seemed to be quieting down. Their dad approached him, his hand outstretched.

"Just put the gun down and we can talk." Ronald's hand shook as he continued to hold the gun. Hector persisted in his approach. Howard tried to slip around the table to get behind him to grab his arm. Their dad reached out his hand to take the gun when Ronald jerked back. "No," he yelled as the gun went off hitting their dad in the shoulder. Ronald screamed and ran out the door.

Howard ran to his dad who sat down at the kitchen table with his hand over the wound on his shoulder.

"Go after him," he told Howard. "I'm okay. It's just a surface wound." George gave him a kitchen towel to stop the blood flow as Howard went out the kitchen door, followed by his mother.

Another shot rang out in the woods. Verna screamed and started to run towards the sound. Howard wrapped his arms around her, holding her back as she cried and fought to be released. Hector came out on the porch, the towel wrapped around his shoulder. George followed in his wheel chair.

"Howard, you keep your mother here," Hector said as he walked down the steps. He walked to the woods calling Ronald's name lest he startle him. There was no sound as he entered the wooded area. The silence was deafening to those waiting on the porch. Hector came back, his face ashen. He told George to go inside with his mother and took Howard aside.

"Call the police and the ambulance," he said.

"Is Ronald okay?"

"Just call them," Hector repeated. Howard made the phone call from the kitchen phone, then joined his dad on the porch.

"You wait out front for them. When they come, direct them back here. I'll be waiting with your brother."

"But," Howard started to protest. His dad held up one hand to silence him. Howard went to the front of the house, going around the house rather than through it lest he have to face his mother.

When the ambulance and police arrived, he directed them back to the woods, following along. Only then did he see his brother, lying on the ground with part of his head blown away. Blood lay about him as the medics pronounced him dead. The police picked up the gun and questioned his father as Howard watched in shock.

"Go, be with your mother and brother," Hector instructed. He remained to deal with the police.

Howard stopped his narration, returning to the present day. Chloe didn't know what to say. Finally she ventured a response.

"How awful for you. I never knew."

"It wasn't something you talked about. You just didn't talk about such things. There was a stigma. No one talked about it. We all said it was an accident even though we knew it wasn't." Howard pushed his plate away, stood up and started to clear the dishes. "That's enough for one night."

"I'll take care of these, Grandpa. You go relax," she told him.

Chapter 15

Northern Ireland, 1947

Mary Helen crossed herself as she whispered the morning blessing to herself in Gaelic. The words felt strange and yet comforting as she prayed them. Words her grandmother had taught her as a child lest the tradition be lost as the language was being lost. As a child, she had begun each day with them but had stopped when she entered her teens. Now, she found herself picking up the prayers again.

Liam had reappeared as quickly as he had disappeared. One night he had just showed up, taking his place in the room set aside for Granda Mike. He gave no explanation, nor was one expected. He found work at the docks along with the O'Connor boys.

Mary Helen continued to enjoy dancing every night. Sometimes Sean walked her home, other times she found her way home with her girlfriends. She stood with her friends sipping soft drinks as the music changed to a slow dance.

"Oh no, here comes one of those dickey dancers," Annie said. "He'll be looking for you, Mary Helen." Mary Helen looked for an escape route. These were the boys who waited for slow dances in order to press their bodies against an unsuspecting girl. Mary Helen and her friends looked for any dancing companion in order to avoid them. If they fancied the looks of you, they would chase you around the floor.

Mary Helen turned her back to the man, hoping to avoid him. When tapped on her shoulder she was prepared to tell off the pursuant, only to see Sean O'Connor standing in front of her.

"Care to dance?" She took his hand without a word and followed him onto the dance floor.

"I was thinking you didn't dance," she stated as the music started. She had seen him at dances before but never on the dance floor.

"I couldn't let Paddy O'Neill take advantage of you. I swore to your brother before he left in the war that I would watch out for you."

"You did now?"

"Aye."

"And what if I don't need watching out for?"

"Well, then, I'm sure Paddy would be happy to take my place."

"I can take care of myself."

"I'm sure you can, Miss Mary Helen." They waltzed across the floor.

"So you can dance," Mary Helen said.

"Everyone can dance."

"But you don't."

"Guess I didn't have the right partner."

"You know I am engaged."

"Engaging, that you are. I hear you do the traditional Irish dance too."

"I love it."

"So you're a traditionalist?"

"What do you mean by that?"

"I'm meaning, what is a traditional girl doing being engaged to an American? Will you really leave your country?" Mary Helen ignored the question. She went back to her girlfriends after the dance without another word.

Chapter 16

"What's that step you do?" Kathleen was watching Chloe put Ashley through her dance steps.

"Which one?" Chloe asked. Even at seven months she was still able to dance, she just didn't kick or jump as high as she used to.

"That slip step."

"Do you mean the slip jig step?"

"I don't know, show me it." Chloe did a quick light step. "Yes, that one. It's different."

"That's because it's just a little off balance. It's in 9/8 signature time. There is an extra beat or a missing beat, depending on how you consider it. It's unbalanced."

"I can relate to that, being unbalanced."

Chloe smiled and shifted her focus back to Ashley. She was enjoying her work at the dance studio even if it didn't pay much. She had planned on getting a waitress job as well to supplement her income but her grandfather had talked her out of it.

"You've got free room and board. Just focus on your dance classes and having a healthy baby." If her mother had told her that, she would have resisted, but coming from her grandfather, it felt like a blessing. After so many years of waitress work in between being in chorus lines, this was a nice reprieve.

She had taken on the job of driving Ashley to dance classes in Plymouth each week. While there she also took instructions from Patrick to prepare herself for teaching someday. Kathleen came along at times to keep them company and check on Ashley's progress.

"Just want to make sure my brother is getting his money's worth." Chloe was aware that Kathleen was also intrigued about all the preparation for the upcoming competition. She would drive to give Chloe a break. Sometimes Chloe filled her in on Howard's stories.

"So, there was someone before Helen. You would never know it from the way he talks."

"That was a long time ago." Chloe wasn't sure how she felt about this "other woman" in her grandfather's life.

"So, you and Sheila?" Chloe had asked as they sat down to dinner the other night, cuing her grandfather to pick up where he had left off.

"Not really."

"I thought you said you had been sweet on her, that you went to movies together."

"We did, but it quickly became clear that it was not meant to be. I had made a promise to Helen, and Sheila wasn't interested in me. She just wanted someone to go to the movies with, nothing serious. But then she introduced me to her younger sister, Betty."

"Was she a nurse too?"

"Studying to be one."

"When did Aunt Sheila start to date Uncle George?"

"I don't know when it officially started. Don't know that they ever 'dated' in the traditional sense. It seemed they just slipped into a relationship, years after Ronald's death. She had been hurt by his death, though you wouldn't know it. Your Aunt Sheila put on a good show, pretended not to care. But I knew differently. As tough as Sheila was, her sister Betty was the opposite. She would come from her shifts as a nurse in training at the hospital and cry. Sheila scolded her, told her she needed to toughen up. At one point Sheila was dating a sailor. We would double date. But he wasn't right for her. I think Sheila knew that. I think she was just trying to get George to take note, show some interest."

"And was he interested?"

"Yes, only he tried to hide it, even from himself. Thought he wasn't good enough for her, him being in a wheel chair and all."

"How did Sheila convince him otherwise?"

"I don't know, but Sheila had her ways. I expect she told him off until he finally got angry enough to propose."

"You think that's how it happened?" Chloe's forehead creased as she imagined the scene in her head. She could see her Aunt Sheila haranguing her uncle, pushing buttons until he finally yelled at her and let slip that he loved her. Her dad had talked about his uncle as being soft spoken and calm. Not much would move him to yell. But if anyone could get a rise out of him, she suspected it was Aunt Sheila. Chloe had only met them through pictures. Still she could see them in a passionate kiss, their first kiss.

"He's not good enough for you," George would say about her latest romance.

"How do you know who's good enough for me?"

"I just know. No one is good enough for you."

"Including you?"

"Especially me. You deserve someone who knows you, the true you beneath that tough exterior, who loves you."

"Like you do?"

"Yes, like I do." In his anger, George let it slip.

"That's all I needed to hear," Sheila said. "I'll be the judge of who's good enough for me." She planted a hard kiss on his lips, waiting for him to respond.

"What's the matter?" she asked. "Aren't I good enough for you?" At this George reached up and pulled her face back down to his, kissing her forcefully and not letting her go. Or at least that was how Chloe imagined it. She had a lot of time to imagine things as she waited for the baby to be born.

However it happened, George and Sheila finally got married in 1949, four years after George came home from the war.

"Grandpa, when did Aunt Sheila die?"

"Way too young. Back in the sixties. Lung cancer. She had only been forty-six. It had been a wakeup call for both your grandma and me. We stopped smoking shortly afterwards, cold turkey."

"I didn't know you both smoked."

"Everyone did back then."

"What happened to Uncle George?"

"He couldn't live on his own. Our mother wanted him to move back in with them but he would have none of it. We offered to take him in, but he was proud and stubborn. He ended up at the V.A., died around ten years later."

"That's sad."

"He had a number of good years with Sheila, some of the best. Life goes on."

"What about you and Grandma?"

"The letters became fewer and fewer. I was busy taking classes at night. Ma was never the same after Ronald's death. She needed me. And there was Betty. I hadn't forgotten your grandma, but it was awful lonely at times. Betty was still in school, working on her degree, taking classes at night, working in the hospital during the day. Neither of us had much time for dating, but what time we had we spent together.

"But I hadn't forgotten your grandmother. It just seemed like we weren't meant to be at times. So many roadblocks. It's hard to keep up a long-distance relationship. I felt guilty about dating Betty. You see, I had made a promise and I keep my promises. I had told your grandma I was coming back for her, so I had to. It wasn't fair to Betty or to Helen the way it was. So I took the money I had been saving for her fare to America and used it to visit her in Northern Ireland in 1949.

"I had planned on telling her about Betty, seeing if any feelings remained between us. But when I saw her, I was smitten again. It was awkward at first. She wasn't the young girl I remembered. She had changed, was somehow harder, I suspect from the hardships of life there. When I talked about marriage, she wasn't ready. Said she didn't know that she could leave her country."

"What did you do then, Grandpa?"

"What could I do? I couldn't move to Belfast, not with my mom the way she was. I had to finish school and help with Ma and George. We agreed that the promise was no longer binding and we were free to pursue other relationships. So I came back, told Betty it was over with Helen, but part of my heart was still hers.

"I continued my schooling, continued dating Betty and saved my money for a home someday, still part of me was in Northern Ireland."

"They say Ireland does that to you. It captures your spirit so you always have to go back," Chloe said.

"Who says that?"

"My dad. He said Grandma had told him that."

"I guess that was the case for me. I didn't know that about your dad. Did he ever take you?"

"He kept promising to take me, but he never got around to it. Mom took me to the dance championships in Dublin, but we didn't have time for seeing the country. All we saw was where the championship was held."

"It would be good for you to go to Northern Ireland. You have family there. Maybe after the baby is born we could go."

"Sounds good to me, Grandpa, as long as you're up for it."

"Why wouldn't I be up for it?" Chloe knew her grandfather hated to be reminded about his age.

"So how did you and Grandma get back together?"

"That's for another time." Howard pulled back his chair from the table and retreated to the living room as Chloe cleared the table.

55

Chapter 17

Chloe was a welcome addition to the dance studio and the dance studio gave Chloe a diversion from her pregnancy and a new group of friends. Chloe knew Letty enjoyed hearing her stories about New York.

"You know, I still have friends there if you ever want to check it out, maybe try out for one of the dance companies," Chloe had suggested.

"Now don't you be stealing my head instructor away," Kathleen had overheard the suggestion.

"Just a suggestion," Chloe said. "No harm meant."

"Don't be putting ideas into Letty's head." Kathleen said.

Chloe knew that Letty was intrigued by the idea. Letty had told her about auditioning for Juilliard years ago and not making it. Chloe had reminded her Juilliard wasn't the only option. Letty wasn't only interested in ballet. She had talked about the Alvin Ailey American Dance Theatre. Chloe enjoyed dreaming with Letty. She could live vicariously through her. It was a nice escape from the reality that was the baby growing ever larger inside of her.

"What about the baby's father?" Kathleen had asked Chloe on one of their trips to Plymouth.

"He's not in the picture."

"Does he know about the baby?"

"Yes, but he's touring."

"With what production? Maybe we could go see him. They get a lot of companies in Detroit and other cities in Michigan."

"I don't know. I don't want to see him." Chloe appreciated Kathleen's understanding. Kathleen had had two sons without the benefit of a father around. She had told her that the men she had dated back then had not been ones she wanted in her life or her sons' lives. Still it wasn't that Chloe didn't want Kevin in her life, more that she didn't know what she wanted.

"Besides, I may give the baby up for adoption."

"Don't do that, Chloe," a voice sounded from the back seat of the car. "I'll help you take care of the baby."

"Why would you do that?" Kathleen asked, ignoring Ashley's protestations.

"I can't raise a baby and dance on Broadway."

"Are you sure you want to return?"

"No, but what else can I do?"

"You can stay here. I'm sure Howard loves having the company."

"But will he still love it when there's a crying baby in the house."

"Trust me, you can trust him. He'll be fine with the baby. He loves my brother's kids."

"But what would I do? I can't just stay home and watch the baby."

"I can't promise you a lot, but you could teach classes. You could teach Irish step dancing."

"And what would Patrick say about that?"

"He doesn't have a say in the matter. Besides, why else is he working with you?"

"It's nice to have options."

"Just don't do anything rash where that baby is concerned. Think about it."

"I'll help take care of the baby." This time Ashley shouted, making her voice heard above the sound of the engine and adult talk.

"I heard you, Ashley. I know I can count on you," Chloe reassured Ashley.

Think about it, Chloe thought. That was all she was doing with so much time on her hands. She thought about it but didn't want to think about it. And she didn't want to think about her baby's father either. Only Letty had been able to get his name out of her.

"You know, he's in the touring production of Wicked that is coming to East Lansing." Letty had looked him up. "Let's go see him."

"I don't know."

"We can see the show then meet him afterwards. Come on, it'll be a fun night out."

"I doubt he wants to see me."

"How do you know unless you ask?" Letty insisted. Chloe remained firm in her refusal to contact him.

"At least let me take you out to dinner. You don't have much time left as a free woman," Letty had coaxed her to go out. "Soon you'll be stuck at home with a baby. Let me treat you."

Chloe had agreed, looking forward to a night out. When she saw Kevin, she regretted her decision. She tried to get up and slip out before Kevin saw her, but Letty stopped her, putting her creamy brown hand on her arm.

"What is he doing here?" she mouthed to Letty.

"It will be okay," Letty's eyes told her. Chloe doubted that but settled back down.

"Isn't this great? I called Kevin and he was free tonight," Letty said.

"Your friend is pretty persistent," Kevin said as he gave her a kiss. "Chloe, you look great." Chloe remained seated, not only because it was hard to get up with all the additional weight, but because she didn't want him to see her like this. "I had been unsure about taking a phone call from this woman I didn't know until she told me she knew you."

"Good to meet you," Letty said as she introduced herself.

"Well, you are pretty persuasive," Kevin stated.

"That she is," Chloe agreed.

"It's good to see you, Chloe. You look great," Kevin repeated. Chloe almost believed him.

"You know I had nothing to do with this. I don't expect anything from you."

"I know … you said that before. Wasn't sure you hadn't changed your mind. What have you been doing?"

"I'm staying with my grandfather until the baby is born, teaching some dance classes. After that, I don't know what. What about you?"

"I finish touring this fall, then I've got a lead on a good part on Broadway. I'll be an understudy. It could be my big break."

"Glad to hear that."

"What about you? You coming back to New York? There might be a part for you in the production I'm auditioning for."

"I can only see as far as having the baby. I'll plan after that."

"You always were able to go with the flow, no obsessing about plans."

"But Letty here, she might be interested in New York." Chloe shifted the conversation away from her, leaving Kevin to work his charm on Letty. He gave her his card before he left.

"If you decide to come to New York, give me a call. I promise I won't make you call ten times before I answer. And you," he turned and addressed Chloe, "Let me know what you decide, if you need anything." Chloe struggled to get up, allowing him to see the full extent of her girth.

"Wow, you look like you could pop any time."

"Not yet, but soon. Now if you'll excuse me." Chloe pushed past him to the rest room.

"Was I right, calling him?" Letty asked on the drive home. "He's not the ogre I thought he might be. I was afraid he wouldn't show up."

"I don't know. It was good to see him."

"Do you think he meant it when he said to call him, about New York?"

"The only way to know is to call him."

"But what about you? This night was supposed to be about you, not me."

"If you mean, did seeing Kevin help me know what to do about the baby, no. It did remind me of what I had given up."

"Was that good or bad?"

"I don't know. I do love dancing. The few times I got a gig, it was great. And New York is great. Hanging out with other starving artists . . . Staying up all night, dreaming of that break. But then waiting on tables, struggling to get by, living in a cramped apartment . . ."

"If you are thinking about adoption, have you talked to anyone yet?"

"No, I haven't done anything."

"You can't just expect these things to work themselves out."

Chloe stared out at the road, not wanting to acknowledge that that was precisely how she ran her life.

"My mom works for United Way. She knows all the local non-profits. She'll know about adoption agencies. Do you want me to ask her?" Chloe continued to stare into the dark.

"Okay," she finally said. Time to take charge of her life, she told herself.

Letty pulled up in front of Howard's house. She faced Chloe, "I know this is hard, but if there is any way I can help . . ."

"You've already helped," Chloe said as she slipped out the door, wiping a tear away from her eye.

Chapter 18

"I hate it when people treat me like a kid." Howard found Ashley sitting slouched over on the floor of the classroom.

"Who treats you like a kid?"

"Everybody."

"Who's everybody?"

"Aunt Kathleen, Chloe."

"Oh, that everyone."

"They treat me like I don't know anything." Howard looked about the room for a chair, found a folding chair, pulled it over and sat down next to her.

"I'd sit down on the floor next to you, but I probably wouldn't be able to get up."

"That's okay, Uncle Howard. You can't help."

"Oh," Howard waited for her to say more.

"Aunt Katherine and Chloe, when we drive to Plymouth, it's like I'm not even in the car."

"What do they talk about?"

"About the baby. Chloe wants to give it up for adoption."

"Oh," Howard hadn't talked to Chloe about this for a while. He had thought Chloe had changed her mind.

"I told her I would help, but she didn't listen. She thinks I'm just a kid."

"Maybe she couldn't hear you."

"I yelled at her."

"Sometimes yelling doesn't work. Sometimes people can't hear you until they are ready."

"When will she be ready?"

"I wish I knew."

"I don't want her to give the baby up before I have a chance to know her."

"Maybe I can help."

"How, Uncle Howard?"

"Would you like to come over for dinner some time? Maybe a sleepover?" Howard leaned over as he made the invitation.

"Can I bring Lucky?"

"Sure. Wouldn't have you come without him." Howard smiled and leaned back on his chair.

"Okay." Howard figured Ashley would welcome the chance to get away from home. Not that it was bad at home, from what he could tell. It just wasn't the same with her mom gone. Ashley had complained about Ava, her dad's new girlfriend, being there all the time. And then there was her pesky brother, Jacob, and even peskier little sister, Grace. Howard and Lucky had come into Ashley's life while her mother was dying from cancer. He had been particularly fond of Ashley and Ashley of him, adopting him as an uncle. He figured Ashley would enjoy a sleepover with Chloe at "Uncle Howard's." It would be good for Ashley and just may be what Chloe needed.

Howard made arrangements with her dad for Friday night.

"We'll pick her up after class and bring her back sometime on Saturday. Oh, and Lucky too."

This wasn't the first time Ashley had come to Howard's home, but it was the first time she stayed overnight. She explored nooks and crannies she had missed before.

"Is that Helen?" Ashley picked up a picture of a young woman in Celtic dress.

"Yes," Howard responded, "back when we first met."

"I thought so. She looks like your story of her." Howard smiled. Ashley continued to look at the pictures on the wall and sitting on tables.

"This is from the war," she stated as she looked at his framed service record. "Who are these men?" She looked at a picture of three men in uniform standing in front of a white house with large front porch.

"That's me and my brothers."

"You didn't tell me you had brothers."

"They died a long time ago."

"Oh." Ashley ran her hand along the surface of the couch, feeling the texture of the fabric. Chloe came in with a bowl of popcorn, followed by Lucky.

"What movie do you want to watch?"

"Why don't you listen to me?" Ashley asked.

"What are you talking about?" Chloe responded.

"Why do you want to give your baby up?"

"I never said I want to."

"Then you don't have to." Chloe looked at Howard for help.

"I think I better take Lucky out," Howard excused himself, leaving Chloe alone with Ashley.

Chloe looked for an exit then realized she had been outmaneuvered. She sat down on the couch and looked at Ashley.

"Sometimes you have to do things you don't want to do. Sometimes you have to do what's best for other people. I have to think what's best for the baby."

"I can help you with the baby. I'll babysit. I'm almost twelve. That's old enough."

"You are only eleven, but you are a mature eleven."

"Eleven is close to twelve," Ashley persisted.

"It isn't just about having help. It's about what's best for the baby. Wouldn't the baby be better off with a real family, a mother and father who love it?" Chloe sighed as she rubbed her stomach.

"The baby will have a real family. She'll have Uncle Howard and you and me and Aunt Kathleen."

"Why do you think it's a girl?" Chloe had refused to know the sex of the baby. It would have made it seem too real.

"I just know."

Chloe stared off into space. It seemed she was doing that a lot lately. She didn't know what to say. She had gone to an adoption agency the other morning with Letty. The people had been very kind. They hadn't pushed her at all. They told her about some couples who were looking for a baby, showed her pictures. The couples had looked so happy in the pictures. They had money she didn't have. They would be able to provide so much for her baby, so much more than she could. And then she could go back to New York. Letty would go back with her. They had talked about it. She wouldn't be alone when she went back. She could look up Kevin and the rest of her friends. She missed them, missed New York. It sounded like the perfect solution for everyone. Then why did she feel like crying?

"A baby girl," she said, still rubbing her enlarged stomach. What would that be like? She didn't know. "I don't know, Ashley. I don't know what I will do, but I promise you, whatever I decide, I'll let you know. I'm sorry you think I don't listen to you."

"That's okay. Adults do that all the time."

"Yes, well, I don't want to be like everyone else. I promise I'll do better. Now what movie do you want to watch?" They were busy, sitting on the couch, eating popcorn and watching Matilda when Howard came back inside with Lucky. "They made the movie into a musical on Broadway," Chloe was explaining to Ashley when he came in.

"Now don't you go filling her head with Broadway," Howard cautioned as he sat down in his recliner for his pre-bedtime nap. Ashley and Chloe laughed and threw popcorn at him, which Lucky ate.

Chapter 19

"Tell me more about what it was like, dancing on Broadway," Letty asked Chloe.

"Nothing quite like it. The energy, the other dancers, I loved it."

"So, other than being pregnant, why did you leave? Are you going back?"

"It's great when you can get a part. Not so great in between parts. And it doesn't pay well. There's no job security, and then there's touring, living out of a suitcase. Okay for me, but not for children."

"Are you going back?"

"Don't know. I haven't decided yet."

"Maybe we could go together. Share an apartment. Go to auditions together."

"And what about the baby? I can't seem to think straight. I would have to give up the baby. I can't decide. I know what my grandfather thinks I should do. I just don't know what I want to do."

Letty was fascinated by the idea of going to New York.

"My parents would freak if I went to New York."

"My parents weren't exactly happy about it."

"Your parents didn't approve, but you went anyway. How could you afford it?"

"Well, I was done with college so I didn't have that expense. My parents had paid for that. So I just went. I told them I had a job possibility. I didn't tell them the possibility was an audition to be in a chorus line."

"What about the dance companies in New York?"

"They are extremely competitive. You pretty much have to either take classes there or know someone to even audition. Besides I had some voice training, too. I was hoping for musical theater, not just dance."

"I know which dance company I would perform with if I ever had the chance." Letty's eyes closed partway as if dreaming.

"Which one?"

"Alvin Ailey. My mother took me to see them when I was little. She also took me to see the Sleeping Beauty Ballet and, of course, the Nutcracker, but Alvin Ailey was the one I remembered the most. They combined ballet with other dance. It was amazing to see so many African American dancers on stage."

"Have you looked into auditions?"

"No, I never told anyone, not even Joy when she talked me into auditioning for Juilliard." Letty remembered that failed audition, Joy's kind words. She hadn't said anything about Alvin Ailey at the time. She knew Joy would have supported her in pursuing this dream. She also knew her parents would have been dead set against it.

"I'm not sure what appealed to me most as a kid. The non-traditional dance movements, the African flare and story within some of the dances or just that there were so many African American dancers. I had never seen that before. I think that was why my mother took me to the performance. She wanted me to be proud of my heritage. She didn't know how much of an impact it had had on me." Letty's parents had struggled to make it out of the ghetto they had grown up in, making it in the white world by their own account through hard work and an education. Now they were comfortably upper middle-class. They appreciated their African American heritage, as long as it was removed by a generation or two from the poverty they had grown up in.

Chloe was busy on her iphone while Letty talked. "Let's see what we can find out about the company." It took some time and effort exploring the web site and other resources but finally Chloe found what she was looking for.

"There's nothing about auditions for the company, but there's another dance company associated with Alvin Ailey, Ailey II. You have to be invited to audition for that company. From there you might be able to advance to the main company."

"So how do you get invited?" Letty moved closer to Chloe to look over her shoulder at the small screen.

"It doesn't say, but it looks like if you take dance classes at their school, you might get noticed and then be invited to audition. Ailey II is a two-year program. It says here it prepares you for a career as a dancer, teacher or choreographer. Some go on to be part of professional dance groups or have careers on Broadway or TV."

"Like I could afford to attend." Letty sat back down next to Chloe. "Not with what I make teaching at the dance studio. The only classes my parents will fund are ones to get my degree."

"It says they have scholarships available."

"My parents make too much money for me to qualify for a scholarship. That's always been the case. The bane of the middle class."

"No," Chloe continued to read. "It says the scholarships are based on performance, not need."

"They are?" Letty leaned over to look at the phone.

"Yes. They have a six-week summer program. You could do that and if it doesn't work out, you still have your position at the dance studio."

"What do I have to do?"

"It looks like you have to go to New York to audition."

"Like I can do that."

"Sure you can. We'll get you one of those budget flights and you can stay with some of my friends."

"Do you think they won't mind?"

"Of course not. They are theater people. We look out for each other. Maybe Kevin will be in New York that weekend. He'll put you up. But if not, I have other friends." Chloe started filling out the application form for her. "Here," she handed her phone to Letty. "You do this."

"What about the application fee?" Letty hesitated. It was all happening so fast.

"That's what credit cards are for."

"Maybe I should think about it some more."

"What's there to think about? It's only an audition."

"Yeah, you're right." Letty finished the information and clicked submit. "There, I did it." She waited for a confirmation, her lips pinched together as she thought about what she had just done. When the confirmation that her application had been received appeared, Letty wasn't sure whether she was relieved or upset. What had she done?

"It looks like they'll be letting you know the date and time for the audition later," Chloe read over Letty's shoulder then took her phone back. "Once we know that, we can arrange for a flight and place for you to stay."

Letty received this information later that week. "Are you sure you can't come with me?" she asked Chloe.

"Like this?" Chloe indicated her belly.

"I know. It just would be easier if I had someone with me."

"You'll do fine. Kevin is going to meet you at the airport. Everything's taken care of." Chloe booked her on the cheapest flight she could find. "The only thing is, not only do they charge you for checked bags, they also charge for carry-ons that go in the overhead compartments. You'll have to pack light. Put everything you need in a backpack and you'll be okay."

Chloe went over everything with Letty. As far as her parents knew, she was spending the weekend in Detroit as she had done on numerous occasions in the past while attending dance workshops. Even Kathleen didn't know.

"We can let her know if you get into the program. She'll be okay with it. She's okay with anything that makes you a better dancer." Still Letty felt guilty about not telling Kathleen about the audition despite Chloe's assurances.

"It's not like you are going to be gone during the school year," Chloe had told her.

The weekend was a whirlwind. Kevin picked her up as he had promised. "Fortunately this was one of our 'dead' weekends." Meaning they didn't have any shows that weekend so he was able to be home in New York. He introduced Letty to his friends. She had a sleepless night on his couch. Not a good way to start the day. Kevin rode the subway with her to the Joan Weill Center for Dance on the corner of 55th Street and 9th Avenue, which housed the school. Kevin waited patiently during the closed audition.

"How'd it go?" he asked when she came out.

"I don't know. I guess it was okay. They asked me a lot of questions afterward about what I was doing, the dance studio, what my goals were."

"That's good. They wouldn't have asked if they weren't considering you."

"You think so?" Letty felt her body start to relax. After twenty-four hours with little sleep, she was existing on adrenaline.

"I know so." Kevin reassured her. "Now that that is over, is there anything you want to do while you are here? I've found after an audition it's best not to keep your mind on it. Best to forget about it. There's nothing else you can do so let it go."

The dance school was located close to the Theater district. "Maybe we can get discounted seats for a show," Letty said. "It doesn't matter what. I just want to see a show." They waited in line to get cheap tickets for a show that night, walked through Times Square and down Broadway before heading home for a nap before going out for the night.

After the show, they met some friends of Kevin's for drinks and a late meal. Kevin ordered a pizza to go as they were preparing to leave.

"How can you still be hungry?" Letty asked as Kevin took out a piece to eat as they walked.

"Dancing is strenuous exercise, you should know that. Got to keep up my carbs. Besides, this won't go to waste." He grabbed one more piece then placed the box next to a bundle of clothes on the sidewalk. Letty was surprised to see the clothes move and a face pop out.

"Yo, Monroe, here's dinner," Kevin said as he woke the sleeping man.

"Kevin, my man. Thank you," the man said as he sat up and opened the box.

"Who was that?" Letty asked.

"Monroe? I met him skateboarding a few years ago. I was working on some new moves. Monroe's an Iraq war veteran. He was a skateboard genius, just can't function in the 'real' world. I make a point of ordering extra pizza whenever I'm out at night and leaving it for Monroe or one of the other street people sleeping on grates in the city." Letty could see why Chloe had fallen for Kevin. He could be charming, especially when he wasn't trying to be charming.

Letty slept late the next day. She hardly had time to get dressed and grab something to eat before getting an Uber ride to the airport. Letty had plenty to occupy her mind while waiting for her flight, sitting on the tarmac and during the flight. Chloe picked her up at the airport, despite Howard's reservations about her driving that far alone. Letty was glad Chloe had insisted that he stay home. Howard was the only other one who knew about Letty's plans.

Letty and Chloe talked non-stop on the drive home, Letty filling in Chloe on what her friends were doing.

"What's wrong?" Letty thought she saw a twinge of regret cross her friend's face.

"I miss New York," Chloe said, "Even though I know I couldn't come given my situation," she patted her stomach, "Still I miss New York. I miss my friends."

When the letter came with the results from the audition, Chloe was the first person Letty called.

"What does it say?"

"I don't know yet. I haven't opened it." Letty fingered the sealed envelope with Alvin Ailey School of Dance on the return label. "It's a thick envelope. Do you think that's a good sign?"

"Just open it," Chloe said, "or I'll come over and open it for you."

Letty slipped open the envelope, read the letter addressed to her and squealed quietly, not wanting her parents to know anything was up.

"I got in."

"I knew you would."

"There's information about school, classes, orientation, fees ..." Letty's voice rolled to a stop when confronted with that reality. "Chloe, I can't afford this."

"What about the scholarship? Does it say anything about that?" Letty shuffled through the papers.

"There's an additional audition for the scholarship, but in the meantime I have to pay $300 to hold my place. It's non-refundable. How can I afford to go back to New York for another audition plus $300?"

"Don't worry, Letty," Chloe assured her. "We'll find a way."

The way was her grandfather. Chloe explained the situation to him.

"Don't you want to support a young dancer in achieving her dreams?" she asked him.

"I don't want to support someone not telling their parents what they are doing."

"Okay, Grandpa. I get your point. I will call my parents."

“Oh, I thought we were talking about Letty.” Howard tilted his head and smiled. “But that would be good.”

“And I’m sure Letty will be letting her parents know.”

“Even better.”

Chapter 20

Northern Ireland 1949

Mary Helen pretended to miss the bouquet her sister threw at her, letting it bounce off her fingertips and into the awaiting arms of the girl standing next to her.

It had been a beautiful wedding. Brigid's best friend had been the maid of honor. Margaret, Mary Helen and Brian's younger sister had been bridesmaids. Margaret's oldest two children served as flower girl and ring bearer while her mother had taken care of the baby. She and Brigid had sewn all of the dresses, using every spare hour they had after work and on weekends. The reception followed in the church hall.

"Why didn't you catch the bouquet? I was thinking you were in a hurry to marry your American." Brigid cornered her afterwards.

"I'm in no hurry." She hadn't told her family about what had happened when Howard came to visit earlier that summer. Couldn't quite bring herself to do it.

Mary Helen remembered the argument with Howard all too well. He had wanted her to move to the states. She replayed the fight in her mind.

"Don't you see, I can't leave my mom right now, not after all she's suffered," Howard said.

"And my mum hasn't suffered?"

"That's not what I meant."

"Why do I have to be the one to give up my home?"

"I thought you wanted to come to America."

"I did, but now . . . I don't know." They had come to an impasse. Mary Helen shook her head in an effort to take her mind away from those thoughts.

"Besides, I can't leave Granny, Mum and Da, can I? Especially now that you are as good as gone," she told Brigid.

"I'll only be a few blocks away."

"Yes, but you'll be living with Brian's family. It won't be the same." Few newly married Catholic couples had the luxury of renting their own home. They had to put their name on a waiting list and live with relatives as they hoped for an opening.

"Is that why you haven't left yet? Because of Mum and Da?" Brigid asked her, breaking into Mary Helen's reverie. Then she looked over to where Sean O'Connor was pouring two glasses of punch. "Or might it have something to do with a certain dock worker?"

"No," Mary Helen insisted as Sean approached with the glasses of punch.

"You look like you could use something to drink," he said as he offered the punch.

"That I can, but it would be a bit stronger than punch." Brigid accepted the glass of punch.

"I can accommodate that as well. Anything for my new sister." Sean pulled out a flask and prepared to pour it into the punch. Brigid stopped him.

"Now don't be ruining good whiskey by pouring it into punch." Brigid drank straight from the flask. Sean offered it to Mary Helen who turned it down as the band struck up a ceili dance, a traditional Irish folk dance. Sean hid the flask back in his pocket and offered his hand instead.

"I didn't know you knew any of the traditional dances," Mary Helen commented as he led her out on the dance floor.

"There's a lot about me you don't know. Are you interested in finding out?" Mary Helen didn't answer, instead focusing on the steps of the dance. Later she saw him in a corner talking to his brother Brian, Margaret's husband, Colin, and her brother Liam. She figured she knew what they were talking about: IRA business. That's all the four of them ever talked about. It had been quiet for the past few years since the end of the war. No fighting. Mary Helen had been enjoying the quiet, but suspected it wasn't going to last.

When Mary Helen came home after the reception her Granny had commented on the wedding. "You'll be next," she added.

"You won't be getting rid of me so soon."

"Whatever happened between you and that American? Thought maybe you would have been going home with him."

"He asked me to."

"Then what's keeping you?"

"And leave you?" Mary Helen teased.

"It's I'll be leaving you, someday, soon."

"Not too soon, Granny."

"Soon enough. Don't be letting me keep you here."

"I'm not."

"Then what is?"

"I don't know, Granny. When I first thought about going to America, it seemed like an adventure. But now I'm thinking on how far away it is. I'll not be seeing any of you."

"That O'Connor boy have anything to do with this?"

"He does go on so about my 'traditional' ways, how I can't leave that part of me."

"You wouldn't be leaving it. You would be bringing it with you. We Irish, we have a history of pilgrimage. All of this life is a journey. Look at all of the stories of saints, how they left home and hearth. Or the monks that left family to live lives of solitude."

"I'm not about to do either of those."

"No, that's not for you. You'll know what's right when the time is right."

Mary Helen appreciated her grandmother's faith in her. If only she had it in herself.

"And anyway, it's over between me and the American. I sent him on his way."

"Oh, you did now," Granny took a long draw off of her pipe.

"Aye," Mary Helen asserted, more to herself than to her grandmother.

USA, 1949

It had been a quiet wedding. George had wanted it that way.

"Why? Because you are ashamed of me?" Sheila had teased him.

"No, I want the world to see my beautiful wife. But how would I get in the church? Now that would be great, me being carried up the stairs into the church by my best men." And so they had a small wedding in his parents' backyard. Howard had been the best man, Betty the maid of honor. They had set up a canopy to protect from rain or sun. They had a cake and punch reception after the ceremony. After the guests had left, Howard turned on the phonograph in the living room, pulled the coffee table out of the way, pushed the chairs and couch back and invited Betty to dance.

"What's a wedding without a few dances? The bride and groom have to have their first dance together and the maid of honor has to dance with the best man." Sheila sat on George's lap as he whirled his wheelchair. When his dad put on a waltz, Howard's smile flickered from his face and he stopped for a moment.

"What's wrong? Don't you know how to waltz" Betty asked. Howard remembered waltzing with Mary Helen. He remembered how she had loved to dance. He shook his head and started to dance.

"Or are you thinking about that Irish girl?" Betty asked.

Howard smiled, "Only thinking about you."

Betty cocked her head and raised her eyebrow but chose to say nothing. George's mother sat by herself in a corner. After the dance he excused himself and insisted Verna dance with him.

"I'm too old for dancing," she protested.

"Nonsense. You are never too old to dance with your son."

"Ronnie's gone, and now George is gone. It won't be long before you are gone too." Verna glanced in the direction of Betty who was dancing with Howard's dad. Betty smiled at them.

"Who's talking about leaving," Howard protested.

"You will. You have to have a life of your own. At least you've got a good American girl." Howard knew his mother had never liked the idea of him being involved with an Irish woman, and a Catholic at that. "Find yourself a good Presbyterian girl," she had told him repeatedly.

"That's not exactly the first qualification I'm looking for in a wife," he had told her.

"What is it you are looking for? Beauty, bah, that fades over time. Just look at me."

"You will always be beautiful to me, Mom." Verna's lips had finally curled in a slight smile. Howard knew how to get her to smile even on her worst days.

"No, you find yourself a Presbyterian girl who knows how to cook to fall in love with," she had insisted.

"Whatever you say, Mom." Betty wasn't Presbyterian, but she could cook. He looked over at her again. Maybe he could make it work.

Chapter 21

Chloe had found a doctor but was none too concerned about all the practical details of having a baby. Maybe if she denied it long enough, it wouldn't be true, she told herself. She did not attend Lamaze classes or read about the birth process. She didn't have a bag packed for the hospital. She would not have had a stock of diapers, baby clothes and other baby items if Kathleen and Letty hadn't insisted upon giving her a baby shower.

"What am I going to do with all of this stuff?" she had asked her grandfather after coming home with her car loaded with baby supplies. Her students had provided her with diapers, bibs, onesies, baby blankets, and clothes. Dale had brought over a crib, stroller, high chair, baby swing and car seat from his children.

"If I need them again someday, I'll know how to find them," he had said when he and Ashley dropped them off. Even Dale's church wanted in on the baby.

"Dale told us about your situation and we wanted to help," two members of the church's woman's group came over with bottles, a diaper pail, more baby clothes and more diapers.

"We'll find a place for all of it," Howard assured. "First we need to set up a nursery in your bedroom, starting with this rocking chair." Howard hauled a rocking chair from the basement. "It was what your grandma used to rock our babies, and then you when you were a baby and came to visit. It's one of the items your grandma just couldn't bear to part with when we moved here. And now you can use it to rock my great grandbaby."

Chloe looked around at the mountain of baby items. "This is going to happen, isn't it, Grandpa?"

"Yes, you are having that baby." He reached over and patted her shoulder, "And everything will be all right."

Chloe finally brought herself to tell her parents on Easter. They had been aware that she was no longer in New York and was staying with her grandfather, but not the reason.

"Oh, and Mom," she paused to prepare herself to spring the news. "I'm having a baby."

"You are? When?" Nora asked, giving herself time to digest the information.

"In May."

"And you are only telling us now?" Chloe hadn't expected a warm response and congratulations. It wasn't exactly good news. She wasn't married, had no means to support herself. She had expected her mom to not be happy, yet that didn't make it any easier to handle her reaction.

"Well, I wasn't sure I was going to keep it."

"We were going to be grandparents and you weren't going to tell us?"

"Grandpa said you should know."

"So, the only reason you are telling us now is because your grandpa insisted?"

"Yes, no, you make it sound so terrible."

"It is terrible. What did I ever do to be treated like this? Jim, talk to your daughter." Nora handed the phone to her husband. In the background Chloe could hear her mother talking to herself.

"So, you know," Chloe said to her dad.

"Something about a baby. It's hard to tell sometimes when your mom gets into a snit." Chloe sure knew about that. She felt better talking to her dad. "So, I'm going to be a grandfather. When?"

"In a month or so."

"You don't give a guy a lot of time to get used to the idea."

"I'm sorry, Dad. I just knew how Mom would be."

"That you do." Jim looked over at his wife who was still ranting. "What about the father?"

"He's not in the picture."

"Do you need help? Money?"

"No, Dad, I'm okay. Grandpa is helping and I've got a part-time job."

"You tell her she's coming home right now." Nora came over to Jim's side. "She needs to come home. We'll take care of everything."

"I don't think she wants to come home," Jim responded, putting his hand over the receiver.

"Of course she does. She just doesn't know her own mind right now. Here, give me that phone." Chloe had heard the conversation despite her dad's attempts to block the words.

"Chloe, darling, we'll come get you."

"No, Mom, I'm staying here with Grandpa."

"But," Nora started. Jim took the phone from her.

"Nora, it's her life."

"What does she know? She doesn't know anything about raising a baby."

"Then she'll learn, same as we learned." Jim removed his hand from where he had placed it on the receiver. "Chloe, you still there?"

"Yes, Dad."

"Whatever you need, you just let us know."

"Thanks, Dad. I will."

"You will let us know when the baby is born," Nora shouted across Jim and into the phone.

"Yes, Mom. I'll let you know," she promised. But not right away, she told herself as she hung up.

The only person she had promised to call first was Ashley. Chloe had been ignoring the pain all morning. Wasn't worse than mild menstrual cramps she had thought when all of a sudden she found herself bent over.

"What was that?" she said as she tried to stand up.

"That, Granddaughter, I believe is labor pain," Howard told her.

"Oh no, it can't be. I'm not ready."

"Babies are born on their own schedule, not ours." He took her hand and helped her stand up. "When did the pain start?"

"Some time last night, but it wasn't enough to keep me awake." Chloe bent over again. "Not like these."

"They seem to be coming quite close together. We better go to the hospital. I'll call your doctor." Howard looked at Chloe as she picked up her cell phone. "What are you doing?"

"Ashley, I promised her I would call."

Dale had just come out of church with his children when his cell phone rang. "Ashley, it's for you." He had refused to let Ashley have her own cell phone. The consequence was having his phone used for her phone calls. "It's Chloe."

Ashley grabbed the phone and turned away from her family. "Chloe?" Dale watched as Ashley listened to the voice on the phone.

Ashley handed the phone back to her dad. "Chloe's going to have her baby. Can I go, Dad?"

Dale looked over at Ava. They had company coming over to the house that afternoon. "I don't know, Ashley," Dale started.

"Maybe I can take you," Ava suggested. She had been dating Ashley's dad for a year but had yet to be accepted by Ashley. Dale knew Ashley only tolerated her for his sake.

"Maybe Aunt Kathleen could take me." Ashley looked at her grandmother who had joined the group. Kathleen made a point of not attending church. "Aunt Kathleen would want to be there."

Esther looked over at Dale before responding. "I'll call her."

"We do have to get ready for our company," Dale said to Ava while Esther called Kathleen. Ava refused to meet his gaze. He knew this wasn't over.

"Kathleen's going to meet us at the hospital. I can take Ashley if that's okay." Esther told Dale and Ava.

Kathleen beat everyone to the hospital. "Seems like old times," she said to herself during the drive. The previous year it had seemed like she was constantly at the hospital. This year she hadn't been there since her son's altercation with a fast moving car last June. She had not missed the place at all. Those other times, Joe had been there as well, in his capacity as pastor caring for his flock. Her mind shifted back to their first kiss, the night Sara's twins had been born. It was not something she wanted to remember. She pushed it out of her head, trying to focus on the matter at hand.

"I wonder if Joe will be here this time," she caught herself thinking as she walked into the emergency room waiting area and glanced about. She didn't know whether she was more relieved or disappointed when she didn't see him. She was thankful to see her mom and Ashley come through the doors, helpful distractions from her thoughts.

Ashley came running, followed by Esther. "Is Chloe here yet?"

"I just got here myself, but no. Chloe hasn't registered yet."

Just then Chloe came in through the doors in a wheelchair pushed by a medical aide. Howard was beside her.

"Here's the welcoming party," Howard said as Ashley ran toward them.

"Are you okay?" she asked.

"Of course I am," Chloe said. "I'm having a baby." She smiled until hit by another sharp pain.

Howard signed her in. As they prepared to take her to labor and delivery a nurse approached the group. "Is the father here?"

"Do any of us look like the father," Kathleen responded.

"Well, then, is there anyone to help Ms. Jones with her labor and delivery?" Kathleen looked at Esther and Howard.

"Don't look at me," Howard said. "I didn't even assist with the delivery of my own children. It just wasn't done back then."

"And I've got to get home," Esther said.

"What do I know about delivering babies?" Kathleen asked.

"You did have two of your own," Esther responded.

"It's just for moral support," the nurse explained.

"Okay, but who will take care of Ashley?"

"Ashley will be fine with me, right Ashley?" Howard said. Kathleen went with the nurse and rode up in the elevator with Chloe to labor and delivery while Howard and Ashley went to the family waiting room.

"Now this is something I know about," Howard said as he took her hand. "I know my way around waiting rooms. Had to wait twice for Helen to have our kids. The first thing we need to do is check out the snack situation." They looked over the vending machines. "Are you hungry?"

"Yes." Ashley had come straight from church and hadn't had lunch yet.

"How about we get something from the cafeteria?"

"Will we miss the baby?"

"Don't worry. These things take time," Howard assured her as they left the room and headed to the cafeteria.

Chapter 22

"She's never going to accept me," Ava said as she and Dale cleaned up after their company had gone home.

"Who?"

"Ashley. She's never going to accept me."

"She accepts you."

"No, she tolerates me for your sake. That's not the same as accepting. Jacob and Grace accept me."

"Give her time. Ashley was older than them when her mother became sick and died. She had more time with her mother."

"That's why she'll never accept me."

"Look, do you want to go to the hospital and pick her up?"

"She made it abundantly clear she didn't want me. She wanted Kathleen."

"Kathleen had been around during Joy's illness . . ." Dale started.

"Yes, I know the story." Ava was getting tired of the constant reminders about Dale's ex-wife.

"Ashley will never have a relationship with you if you don't spend time alone with her."

"I know, but today isn't the day to push it. She doesn't want me. I don't want to force the issue." It was hard, trying to figure out where she fit in this ready-made family. Ava couldn't have children of her own. That made it all the more important to her to be accepted by Dale's children. She had been able to win over Jacob and Grace. Jacob was so easy going. He accepted anyone and everyone. And Grace, well Grace was so young when Ava came into her life. Ava had been able to easily slip into a mother role with her.

Ava thought back over the past year, since she had started dating Dale. She remembered so many good times with Grace and Jacob, taking them for ice cream, going to the park, movies, dinners at their house and tucking them in bed. Ashley had come along begrudgingly, when she wasn't able to find an excuse to stay home or doing something else.

Ava had tried to establish a routine with Ashley, tried to create moments with her, letting her stay up after Grace and Jacob were in bed, as befitting Ashley's status as the oldest.

"What would you like to watch?" Ava invited her to sit on the couch with her and watch a video, patting the seat next to her. "Your choice, whatever you want."

Dale looked up from the papers he was going through and glanced at Ashley. Ashley saw this but looked away.

"I'm going to read in my room," she told Ava and slipped upstairs.

"Guess I might as well be going too," Ava said, getting up from the couch.

"She'll come around," Dale had assured her as he walked her to her car.

"Will she?" Ava looked up and saw Ashley's face watching from her bedroom window. Ashley quickly slipped out of the window, aware that she had been caught. Ava slid into her car, returned home to her empty apartment and tried to lose herself in grading homework assignments.

Ava sighed as she remembered this and other incidents throughout the year. Where Ashley was concerned, it seemed she accepted everyone but her. Ava could understand her preference for Kathleen, after all she was her aunt and had been a surrogate mother to her during her own mom's illness. But now there was Chloe. Who was Chloe to her? Ava didn't understand why Ashley took such a liking of Chloe and not of her.

"Chloe is her teacher," Dale had said when she had mentioned it to him. "And she's a dancer from New York."

"I know, I know, little girls are fascinated with older yet young women for role models. I was a little girl once myself." How could she compete with a twenty-something dancer, her with her thirty-something body?

"Give her time. When we marry, you'll have more time with her."

"If we marry. You haven't exactly asked me yet."

"And would you say yes?"

"You won't know till you ask." Dale may not have asked, but they had talked around it before. All indications were that that was where they were heading. All the more reason to worry about Ashley accepting her.

"How did you end up here?" Chloe asked when left in a room with Kathleen.

"It was either me or your grandfather. I thought another woman might be helpful."

"You think," Chloe tried to smile but grimaced in pain instead. "Maybe I should have taken those classes."

"I don't know about classes, but I do know there are some pretty fine drugs to take care of the pain if you want them."

"But won't that interfere with the labor?" Chloe had read enough to know about the pros and cons of using drugs during labor. "I'll see how it goes, then decide," she told Kathleen. They settled in for a long haul.

It was after eight before the baby was born. Kathleen had called Letty earlier in the day to let her know Chloe was in labor. Letty had joined Howard and Ashley in the waiting room where they played cards to pass the time.

"This is taking forever," Ashley complained.

"Babies come when they are ready," Howard explained.

Ava waited while Dale called Kathleen to check on Ashley. When he wasn't able to reach Kathleen he called Howard.

"How's Ashley? And where's Kathleen?" she heard him ask.

"Ashley's doing fine. Kathleen's in the delivery room with Chloe. No baby yet," Dale repeated to her what he had been told.

"Kathleen in the delivery room?" Ava asked. "I didn't expect that."

"Me neither. Maybe I better go get Ashley," he said.

"Go ahead. I'll take care of Jacob and Grace." Ava had them put their pajamas on and prepared to read them a bedtime story.

"Why does Ashley get to stay out so late?" Jacob complained. "It's a school night for her, too."

"She's waiting to see Chloe's baby."

"I want to see the baby, too. Why can't I go with Dad to see the baby?"

"Me too," Grace echoed.

"Because, Ashley is older than you."

"It's not fair," Jacob whined.

"I know, I know Jacob. Life isn't always fair," Ava tried to settle them down with no luck.

"I want Dad," Jacob continued to whine. "Why can't I go with Dad?"

"I want Daddy," Grace started to whine as well, following her brother's example.

"He's not here and it's time for you to go to bed," Ava insisted, leading Grace upstairs with one hand while Jacob refused to climb the stairs.

"I'm going to stay up until Dad gets home," he insisted.

"You can do that, in your bedroom. Now get up these stairs," Ava told him.

"You can't make me. You're not my mom," Jacob said. Ava had no question about where he had gotten that from. Ashley's influence.

"No, I'm not, but your dad left me in charge." When she finally got them both in bed, she flopped down on the couch.

"Maybe being a mother isn't all I thought it would be," she thought, only to hear cries for a drink of water coming from Grace. "Maybe Ashley isn't the only problem."

"I can't go home yet, Dad. Chloe hasn't had her baby," Ashley said as her dad walked in the door. "Can't I stay with Uncle Howard?" Ashley slid next to Howard.

Howard looked from Ashley to Dale. He didn't want to get caught between the two. "It's up to your father, Ashley."

"We can wait a while longer, but you've got school tomorrow," Dale said.

"Jones?" a nurse called. Howard got up, followed by the rest of the group.

"You've got a baby girl," she told them. "Mother and daughter are doing well."

"Can we see them?" Howard asked.

"In just a few minutes," she said.

Kathleen was holding the baby when they went back to Chloe's room. Chloe's hair was damp from perspiration, her face exhausted, but she was smiling. Kathleen handed her the baby.

"She's beautiful," Chloe whispered.

"Yes, she is, just like her mother. Have you decided on a name yet?" Howard asked.

"Yes, Mary Helen, after Grandma," Chloe said.

"She would have liked that." For a moment, it was as if she were present in the room with them, then the moment was gone, like so many moments in his life. Howard wanted to hold on to them but they were vapor, disappearing between his fingers when he grabbed for them.

Ashley stood beside Howard, unsure what to do.

"Come here, Ashely," Chloe called Ashley to her. "I can't believe you waited all this time."

"It wasn't so bad. I played cards with Uncle Howard." Ashley reached out to touch the baby's hand. "She's so red and wrinkly."

"That's because she's fresh from heaven," Howard told her. Dale and Letty took their turns coming forward to see the baby, then Dale took Ashley home.

"Are you going to be okay?" Kathleen asked. "Do you need someone to stay with you?"

"You can go home, all of you," Chloe said. "I've got plenty of help."

"Are you sure? I can stay for a while," Letty offered.

"And watch me sleep? No need for that," Chloe said. "Grandpa, you look tired. Someone make sure my grandpa gets home," she instructed

"I'll be fine," Howard said. "I'll see you in the morning. Take care of my granddaughter," he instructed the nurses on his way out.

"It's been a long day," Kathleen said as they rode the elevator down together. Howard could see she was tired.

"You did well," he told her.

"Did I? I've never been a surrogate father before. Never seen a baby be born or been part of a delivery. I have two sons, but that had been in a drug-induced haze."

"I'm sure you did just fine, and my granddaughter would say the same thing if she were here."

"What about you? Do you need a ride home?" Kathleen asked him.

"Never been better," he assured her. Never been better, he repeated to himself.

At last, Chloe was alone with her daughter. She fought sleep as she looked at the dozing infant, smiled as she moved ever so slightly and made a light, cooing sound. So this is what it is to be a mother, Chloe thought. She's so small. She pushed the call button and had the nurse take the baby so she could sleep. What would she do when there were no nurses to call?

Chapter 23

Northern Ireland, 1950

The men had been banished to the street, leaving the women the run of the house as they ran up and down stairs and through the kitchen. Margaret, having had three children already and another on the way was allowed to assist the midwife. Mary Helen was relegated to heating water and bringing clean cloths. She listened to her sister's cries and vowed she'd never put herself through that.

"There's a reason we don't let women who have never given birth into the birthing room," Granny teased her later when she complained. "We don't want to scare them off." Granny smiled as she puffed on her pipe. Mary Helen didn't see the humor in the situation.

"The first time I assisted at a birth, it was for me own ma. It was late, the midwife barely made it in time. But Ma had already had eight kids. She was an expert by then. The babies just popped out. There was no time to round up other women so I had to help. That was your Uncle Gus." Granny delighted in telling the tale. "I was the first in the family to lay eyes on him, ugly, wrinkly faced boy that he was, screaming at the midwife."

"The one hiding in France?"

"Yes, it wasn't safe for him here after the war. It's still not safe for him to come back." Mary Helen wondered exactly what he had done to warrant such treatment, but as to that, Granny was silent, as she was about any story related to the doings of the IRA.

"Better you don't know," was all Granny would say.

Like the good Catholic girl she was, Brigid was one year married and already a mother. After the mid-wife cleaned him up, Mary Helen swaddled the baby in fresh linen and handed him to his mother.

"A fine boy you have," the midwife stated. Brigid smiled wanly after the exhausting labor. "Don't worry. The first ones are always the hardest. The next will be easier."

Mary Helen didn't find that a comfort.

She went downstairs to the street where Brian, Sean and their father had gathered with some of the neighbors.

"It's a boy," she told them. They slapped Brian on the back and offered him some whiskey.

"Slainte!" they toasted each other.

"I'll be bringing you upstairs to see your wife and child if you are done with all this foolishness," Mary Helen told him. Afterwards she went home to tell the news.

"A fine, healthy boy. A blessing," Granny said.

"What blessing? Another boy to be shot in someone else's war," Mum said. "A curse." Mum had refused to come when summoned.

"You go, Mary Helen. I've had enough of babies," she had said and remained in her chair.

"You don't really mean that?" Mary Helen asked.

"We labor to bring boys into this world, raise them only to be slaughtered in wars. Better to have never born a son," she uttered and went upstairs.

"Don't listen to her," Granny said. "Every child is a blessing from God."

Mary Helen was eager to visit Brigid and the baby on her way home from work the next day.

"Someday, you'll have a wee baby of your own," Brigid told her as she soothed the boy.

"After what I heard yesterday, I'm in no hurry."

"It's not so bad, Mary Helen, and then you have a wee one to care for."

"And feed and clothe and worry about. No, thank you."

"When are you and Sean getting married?" Brigid asked.

"Seems you know more than me. Who says we'll be marrying?"

"It's expected. You've been seeing each other for a year now."

"He's been keeping company with me and the IRA. The IRA is his first love. I'm in a poor second."

"Now don't go on like that. You know it's not our business. It's best we don't know what they are up to."

"Is that what Brian tells you? I'll not have a husband who's gone for days at a time, sneaking out at all hours of the night."

"At least he's not sneaking out with another woman."

"I don't know which would be worse." She reached over and took the baby's small hand in hers. "Brigid, tell me. What are they up to? I've been hearing of plans."

"Even if I knew, I wouldn't tell you. It's best we don't know. None of us."

"I don't understand the appeal of the IRA."

"I think for Brian, it was inevitable."

"What do you mean?"

"His upbringing and background. And then, there's the excitement in it. Raids, arrests, secret parades, arms classes and sometimes public parades challenging authority."

"I don't see the attraction in that."

"Don't you? I thought you more than anyone would understand that. You always were the rebel."

"But that was different. That was rebelling against Mum."

"You loved excitement and a good fight."

"Aye, that I did."

"And now you love an IRA rebel. Seems almost inevitable to me."

"Not to me. I'm not one to stay in the dark at home while my husband goes off on adventures."

"If that's what you call it. Brian calls it his duty. Best we leave them alone to do what they need to do."

That wasn't enough for Mary Helen. She wanted to know where Sean was those nights he didn't come to the dance hall. She wanted to know where Liam was sneaking off at night, coming in as she was lighting the morning fire.

"Nothing for you to worry about," Sean told her. That only caused her to worry more. They had been keeping company for a year now, if you don't count those years before when she had still been semi-engaged to Howard and Sean had walked her home. She had never meant to fall in love with this man. At first she had figured it was just the fact that he had been her brother Jimmy's friend. It had been flattering to have someone so much older than her, paying her attention even though she knew nothing would come of it. After all, she was almost spoken for, she had reminded herself. But then the letters were fewer and fewer, and years passed. She had wondered if Howard would ever return for her. Perhaps it had just been one of those summer romances, or those war romances, that never led anywhere. At least she hadn't been left with a child like some of her friends had.

And then, when Howard did come to see her, she didn't know what the problem was. He had been kind, always a gentleman. They had argued, but there hadn't been much fire in it. Not like how it used to be between her mum and dad, before Jimmy died. She wasn't sure what she wanted. She had been sad when he left, but life went on as it always did. And then there was Sean. He had a way of angering her so that her blood boiled. She wasn't about to be his girl, even after she was free to date. She had tried dating other men from the neighborhood, but none of them set her heart afire the way Sean did.

What was wrong with her? She had had a good man who loved her and she had sent him away. She hadn't been ready to leave her home for him, not then, not now, maybe never. She guessed she hadn't loved him enough. And if she wasn't going to leave her country, maybe there was someone for her here.

With Brigid engaged to Brian and now married, it seemed Brian and his brother were always around. Sean was the older of the two. That made the attraction all the greater. Sean was tall, with a dark complexion, black hair and a smile that lit up his brown eyes. Howard had been shorter, had light brown hair, blue eyes and a fair complexion. Sean's muscles rippled beneath his shirt from all of his manual labor and the hard work on the docks. Howard had been skinny under his uniform. Howard was studying to be an engineer; Sean would most likely never be more than a dock worker. There was no comparison between the two, that different they were. Yet she found herself assessing each, not quite ready to give either of them up entirely.

She focused on Sean's smile as they walked home from a movie, laughing and sharing a cigarette.

"You should have been there back in '43," Sean commented.

"Been where?"

"Back when we took over the cinema."

"You had been part of that?" Mary Helen remembered hearing about it from her friends. A group of IRA had taken over the Broadway Cinema on Holy Saturday and a slide was flashed on the screen: "This cinema had been commandeered by the Irish Republican Army for the purpose of holding the Easter Commemoration for the dead who died for Ireland." Jimmy Steele, a leader of the group, read the 1916 proclamation of freedom from the stage, followed by Hugh McAteer reading a statement of IRA policy for the coming year.

"We concluded with a minute of silence for the dead." Sean paused and took a puff of his cigarette as he remembered. "I had guarded the exit to make sure no one left. We all got away safely."

"Yes, then, but you were thrown in prison after that, weren't you?"

"That was for something else."

"How did you get involved in the first place?"

"Remember Eoin MacNamee?"

"No."

"I was part of the 'belt and boot' brigade he organized. Despite what you may think, most of what we did was shooting in fields, holding drill sessions with old weapons and talking. Not much."

"Not enough to land anyone in jail."

"Sean," a voice came out of the alley.

"Colin, that you?" Sean stared in the dark.

"Aye," the voice answered.

"What are you doing here?"

"You have to come with."

"I have to walk my girl home first."

"No time for that. You have to come now."

Sean looked at Mary Helen. She shook her head, then said, "I'll be okay." He kissed her before running down the alley with Collin.

Chapter 24

"There's Scott," Kathleen pointed him out amidst the procession of black gowns entering the gymnasium. She couldn't believe this was happening. First Josh, now Scott. Her two boys high school graduates, soon to be on their own. Josh was finishing his sophomore year at college. Scott planned to attend the local community college for an associate's degree before entering a trade school. He was going to be working in her brother Dale's plumbing business while going to school.

How did she get such responsible, dependable sons? She, who had been far from responsible most of her life. Not that she took any credit for it. That credit went to her mother who had raised her boys into their teens. The most she could take credit for was having good genes to pass on to her boys.

When she had returned to Cascade Falls five years ago, she had figured she'd stay until her boys were grown and on their own. Now that Scott was soon to be independent, maybe she could think about moving. It had not been her idea, being in charge of an arts center or dance studio. That had all been Joy's idea; Joy's way of trapping her in this town. But it hadn't been so bad. It gave her something worthwhile to do with her life. Far better than running drugs, if less monetarily rewarding. Still something was missing. She was finding it hard to settle down. Her feet longed to travel, seek out adventure. There wasn't a lot of that as far as she could tell in her home town.

"Adventure isn't all it's cracked up to be," she could hear Joy telling her. "I had adventure, touring with Ballet Magnificat, but after a while, all the cities began to look the same. Having children was a greater adventure."

"That's easy for you to say," Kathleen thought, "You're gone now, leaving me with a building to maintain."

"You've said it yourself many times," Joy reminded her. "The dance studio and center are on firm ground. You could find someone to take your place and be free of it. So why don't you?"

"Good question," Kathleen repeated to herself. "Why didn't I leave?" she asked herself again.

"It wouldn't have anything to do with a certain pastor?" Joy asked. Kathleen looked across the bleachers to the floor where Pastor Joe was sitting with Michelle.

"If anything he would be a reason to leave. Clearly my options here are limited. Why else would I even consider dating someone like him?"

"Is that what you think?"

"Yes, it was a mistake, a slip up like most of my relationships."

"If you say so."

"I do say so," Kathleen said, not realizing she had left her internal dialogue and uttered the words out loud.

"What did you say?" Esther asked.

"Nothing, Mom. Just thinking out loud."

Kathleen stood outside with her mom, stepfather, son Josh, and Dale and his family after the ceremony, waiting for Scott to join them for pictures.

"Get a picture of me and Stephanie, Mom." Scott flagged down Stephanie. She came followed by her dad, Michelle and her two sets of grandparents.

"Sure, Scott." Kathleen took the pictures, then the mandatory introductions ensued before Scott and Stephanie excused themselves.

"We want to get ready for the Senior party," Scott said as he prepared to leave.

"Don't stay out too late," Kathleen said.

"Mom, it's an all-night party."

"Oh, yeah. Force of habit," she said as she kissed him before he headed out. "Be careful," she muttered but he was already gone.

"Time for us to go as well," Joe's parents and in-laws said their good-byes. "We will be seeing you at Stephanie's open house, won't we, Kathleen?" Joe's mom added.

"Oh, sure, I guess," Kathleen squirmed as she gave her a hug.

"Nice to finally meet you," she said in Kathleen's ear.

"What was that about?" Kathleen took Joe aside after they left.

"My mom has this strange idea that we are still dating."

"You told her we had broken up."

"Many times. Mom has her own ideas about things. I don't know what Stephanie has been telling her."

"Okay, I guess," Kathleen shook her head then added. "About the graduation open houses . . ."

"Don't worry. We can make a pact. I won't go to Scott's and you don't have to go to Stephanie's."

"That would be silly. Our kids are friends. Our families are friends. There's no reason why we can't be friends." She stretched out her hand to him.

"Friends then," Joe said as he shook her hand.

"See," Kathleen told the voice of Joy in her head. "Just friends."

"If you say so," the voice responded.

Chapter 25

Chloe was excited about Ashley's round of competitions coming up over the summer. There was a feis every month if you were willing to travel. The school of Irish dance Ashley attended focused on ones that were within easy driving distance in Michigan and Ohio. Ashley was scheduled to compete in the Detroit Feis in June, the Great Lakes Feis in July and the Michigan Feis in September, all in preparation for the Mid-America Oireachtas that would be held in November in the Chicago area. An oireachtas, or gathering, is a qualifying event for those who want to participate in the World Irish Dance Championship during Easter Week. The only problem was that Chloe couldn't be there with her. Having had her baby just a few weeks ago, she still wasn't getting around like she used to.

"I'll be there in July," she had promised Ashley. She figured Ashley would hold her to that promise.

There had been no talk of adoption since the night Ashley had stayed over. Chloe still dreamed of dancing again on Broadway, but the dream had been put aside for a while. Like so much of her life, it seems that once again she had made a decision by not making a decision. Once the baby girl had a name, there was no way she could give her up for adoption. But perhaps there could be another way that she could dance and still raise her baby. Others had done it.

Chloe couldn't wait to hear how Ashley was doing. She had been texting Kathleen throughout the competition. Howard had stayed home to help with the baby. Ashley had visited while she was in the hospital after the baby's birth, but hadn't been able to make it over since then because of school and rehearsals. Her grandfather helped as he could. Then Chloe's mother showed up.

Nora came crashing back into her life like a tornado unchained. She set up camp in Howard's home, taking over the basement as her own spot, and turning the quiet household upside down. Chloe had little energy to wrest control from her mother as Nora dictated feeding schedules, bathing schedules, even diaper-changing schedules. Chloe found herself turning over all aspects of her daughter's life to her mother. She nursed Mary when instructed, burped her then handed her back to Nora.

"You rest," Nora instructed. "I'll take care of everything." For once, those words sounded good to Chloe. She had spent so much of her life resisting her mother's controlling nature. But how to resist someone who was larger than life, who filled the room with her presence so that no one else existed? All of her friends had loved her mother.

"You don't have to live with her," Chloe had told them when they raved about her.

"But she's so much fun."

As a child she had only existed as an extension of her mother. She had fought it at times, other times just gave in and went with the flow. Her decision to stop competing in Irish dancing had been her first major step towards independence from her mom. Nora had loved the hair, the make-up and the elaborate costume. At one time, as a small child, Nora had entered her into beauty pageants, but when Chloe failed to win, her mother shifted her focus to dance lessons. If not a beauty queen, then her daughter could be a dance queen. Nora loved dressing her daughter in tutu's and dance costumes. She had a closet at home just for all of Chloe's old dance costumes. It had been a welcome escape for Nora from her humdrum life as a nurse and housewife. She poured all her energy into her one child, her daughter.

For her part, Chloe found she liked dancing and so she put up with all of her mother's machinations. For his part, her father found a way to live with his flamboyant wife.

"She brings drama and color into a dull world," he used to say to Chloe. As long as she confined her attention to her daughter, Chloe knew he was fine to sit by and do nothing. It was only when she directed her energies in his direction that he dug in his heals and refused to budge. He had been Chloe's sole supporter when she had decided to stop competing in Irish dance.

"Let the girl be," he had told his wife as she fumed. "It's her life." Nora, however, continued to treat it as the ultimate betrayal but had to give in before the united front of her husband and daughter. Chloe and her dad had a secret pact. On the surface, they agreed to let Nora have her way, but between them, they knew it was only because they let her.

Chloe had loved escaping her mother's reach each summer as she spent weeks with her grandparents. Her mother and her grandmother had butted heads from the start. No one was good enough for grandma's one and only son, grandma had told her. Grandma had never been able to understand what her Jimmy saw in Nora.

"Leave the boy be," she remembered Grandpa telling her as she fumed. "It's his life, his wife." The two never got along, causing a rift between the families. Her mother would have happily cut all contact between her and her mother-in-law but this was one of those occasions where her dad had put his foot down.

"You're a mother's boy," her mom used to taunt her dad until he let her know this would not work. Her dad was not going to tolerate any unkind words about his mother.

"And if I am a mother's boy, what's it to you? My mother is a saint," he would say, knowing it would cause her mom to fume and refuse to talk to him for days. Her dad appeared to like the peace and quiet.

But if her mom didn't talk to her father, she would vent all of her frustrations on her daughter.

"Your grandmother, the saint. Mark my words, Chloe, never marry an Irish man. You'll always be playing second fiddle to his mother." Chloe hadn't known at the time what playing second fiddle meant, but she figured it was bad. She didn't see what was so bad about Irish men, after all her father was second generation Irish, and so, she quickly fell for an Irish dancer once on her own in New York.

Chloe had had good reason to not let her mother know where she was or that she was pregnant. She figured Nora would barge in and take charge, as she had. At her grandfather's insistence, she had called her parents at Christmas and let them know where she was, but not about the baby. For that she had waited until Easter. Chloe had figured her mother suspected something was up, but she chose to let her imagine the worst as was her wont.

"You have to tell them sometime," she remembered arguing with her grandfather.

"Isn't it enough that I told them where I was?"

"No, it's not. You have to tell them about the baby."

"Not if I decide to give the baby up for adoption. They needn't know at all."

"Even if you decide to give the baby up. They need to know they have a grandchild." Chloe knew her grandfather had hated it every time she brought up the possibility of giving the baby up. "This isn't a game. This is a life you are talking about. Don't talk so lightly about giving up a child. If your grandmother were here . . ."

"But she's not, Grandpa, and I have to make the best decision that I can. Maybe I'm not fit to be a mother. My mother didn't exactly qualify for mother of the year."

"Whatever problems you have with your mother, she's still your mother. She did the best she could, which is all any of us can do. And she loves you."

"Does she? Or does she love the thought of being a mother more than the actual being," Chloe had said and walked away, leaving her grandfather to his own thoughts.

Howard hadn't known what to say. What was it about mothers and daughters? Helen and their daughter had fought as well and now Meghan lived thousands of miles away. They had parted company when Meghan left for college on the West coast.

"Don't be a stranger," Howard had said as he left her at her UCLA dorm room, but he knew the visits would be infrequent, Christmas and summer vacation when school was out. Then Meghan found a job and attended summer session so they didn't even see her then. The cost of a flight was such that neither made the trip on a regular basis, neither he and Helen to visit her, nor Meghan to visit them. He had always made family a priority, so had Helen. Family, their desire to stay close to family, had almost permanently broken them up. And now, here he was with an alienated daughter and daughter-in-law.

Meghan did come more frequently when her mother's illness progressed. And now that Helen was gone, she had invited him to live with her, but it wasn't the same as having children close at hand, within the same town. Things were different from his generation.

Jimmy had been the light of his mother's eyes. Helen had named him for her deceased brother and had doted on him as every Irish mother did. She had never accepted that another woman could take him away from her.

Then there had been grandchildren, first Meghan's two boys, then Chloe. Meghan's boys had lived so far away and Meghan had been reluctant to send them for the summer, but Chloe had been different. From the start there had been a bond between them. As soon as she was old enough to be gone from home she would come and stay, first for a week at a time, later, as she got older for a month or more. Helen had loved those times, as had Howard. She had been a breath of fresh air in their old age. When Helen started to show signs of the progression of her Alzheimer's, Chloe had been good with her, acting more mature than her years. The visits became shorter as she got older and had friends she didn't want to leave and summer jobs. They didn't see much of her during college. Still, she would call and let them know how she was doing. Even once she moved to New York they received the periodic phone call.

"My dad, he was named after Grandma's brother, the one who died during the war, right?" she had asked him during one of their meals.

"Yes, your great uncle Jimmy. There were many lives lost."

"Wonder why Dad never visited Ireland. He used to talk about it."

"He had wanted to go after high school but that was during the troubles in Northern Ireland. We didn't think it was safe."

"What was 'the troubles?' Was it ever safe in Belfast? I've heard about car bombs."

"It's safe now, but during the seventies it was a war zone. There were Catholics killing Protestants, Protestants killing Catholics. It's peaceful now, but the memories remain. Your grandmother visited now and then. She would come home with stories of lives lost, houses burned. Your grandmother's home in Whiterock had been burned during the troubles. Her parents had to stay with Grandma's sister's family until it was restored. She talked of barricades and curfews. Young Irish Catholic men were being taken off of the streets and brutally murdered. They called them the Shankill murders. There was no way your grandma was going to let her son go back then. I don't know why he didn't go later, after the peace accord."

"Guess he was busy with me then."

"Yes, you were just a girl back then."

"And then there was his job. I don't know why he didn't come with us to the World Championship in Dublin, but there was no time for sightseeing. We attended the competition and came home. The competition was a world unto itself."

"Your mother may have had something to do with it. She was always insisting they didn't have enough money, pushing your dad to work more hours."

"I thought the long hours were his way of escaping mom."

"Most likely a little of both. I don't know much about his life since he moved so far away. Not like my day when families lived in close proximity to each other and three generations would share a home."

"It hasn't been like that for a long time, Grandpa."

"I guess not, more's the shame," Howard said as he stood up to clear the table, giving Chloe a break.

Howard had not been happy to have Nora invade his space, but what was he to do? A daughter needs her mother at times like this, he told himself. Helen had wanted her mother back when Meghan had been born. She butted heads with her mother, but wanted her mother. That seemed to be her way. She butted heads with everyone she encountered, including him. But they were pleasant encounters in his memory. They had brought them closer as she was as quick to laugh as she was to get angry. She kept life interesting. And she definitely knew how to get her way where he was concerned.

"Grandma was proud of you and your dancing. We would have come to the championship but already it was starting to be difficult for her to leave home. She would get upset and confused in unfamiliar places."

"I know, Grandpa. You and Grandma were always my biggest supporters."

Chapter 26

Dale knew Ashley couldn't wait to show Chloe her awards. He drove her over on Sunday afternoon. When they got there they were greeted by Chloe's mother.

"She's nursing the baby and can't have any visitors," Nora said.

"We'll wait," Dale told her.

"After she's done nursing, she'll need a nap."

"She'll see me." Ashley spoke up.

"We won't stay long. Ashley wants to show Chloe her awards," Dale said. "Where's Howard? He knows us."

"He's not available," Nora started to say as Howard joined them.

"What are you doing? Trying to chase away my company?" Howard asked.

"Chloe needs her rest," Nora stated.

"Let's let Chloe decide that for herself." Howard pushed Nora aside and invited Ashley and her dad in. "Ashley is always welcome here," he added, smiling at Ashley.

"What's all the commotion?" Chloe walked out of her bedroom, burping Mary on her shoulder.

"Here, let me take the baby," Nora reached for Mary.

"She's fine, Mom. I'm fine," Chloe said, though the shadows under her eyes said something else. Chloe sat down on the couch so Ashley could sit next to her.

"Can I hold her?" Ashley asked.

"You sure can, just make sure you support her neck." Chloe gently placed Mary in Ashley's arms while Nora looked on with a look of disapproval and concern. Ashley looked up at her dad and smiled.

"She's so little," she said.

"Yes, she is. She's beautiful," Dale told Chloe. He sat down across from them, all the while aware of Nora hovering in the background.

"So, tell me about the feis," Chloe said. In her excitement over holding the baby, Ashley had almost forgotten why she was there. She had gotten to see the baby in the hospital, but had not yet held her.

"I won," she said. Dale showed Chloe Ashley's awards, one first place and a second place. "And I passed all my grades!" Grades were a way to show your dance proficiency beyond competition. There were twelve grades. You could take three grades at a time but had to pass the first before going to the next. Ashley had passed the first three grades.

"That's wonderful, not that I'm surprised," Chloe said.

"I wish you could have been there."

"Me, too. I'll be at the next one."

"Don't you think it's time for your friends to leave?" Nora interrupted.

"Oh, I guess. I am tired," Chloe agreed reluctantly with her mother. "But come back soon," she added.

"It's time for your nap." Nora took Mary from Ashley's arms. "Both of you." Nora indicated Mary and Chloe.

Ashley's eyes showed her surprise at Chloe's acquiescence. She looked at Chloe, expecting her to say more but when she didn't, Ashley stood up and looked at her dad.

"We'll come again, when you've had more time to regain your strength," Dale said as they made their goodbyes.

"Come again," Chloe echoed as they left. Howard followed them out to their car.

"Don't you worry about Chloe. She'll be feeling more herself soon," Howard told Ashley. "You know you are always welcome, both of you." Howard said as Ashley climbed in the car.

"Who was that lady?" Ashley asked on the ride home.

"I think that was Chloe's mother," Dale replied.

"I don't like her."

"She wasn't too friendly. Hey, how about I treat my award-winning dancer to some ice cream." Dale tried to lighten the mood. Ashley agreed to the ice cream but continued to wonder about Chloe.

"She didn't seem like herself," Ashley said as she ate her double fudge Sundae.

"Who?" Dale asked.

"Chloe." She didn't say anything more.

"She'll be okay. It's hard having a baby and then adjusting to taking care of the baby. It's good that her mother is here to help her."

"I don't like her," Ashley repeated as she finished her ice cream.

"So, Nora, I imagine you'll be needed back at home soon. Jim must be missing you," Howard said that evening over dinner.

"Jim's fine. I have nothing to keep me from helping with my grandbaby," Nora said as Chloe struggled to eat while holding the baby. "Here, give her to me so you can eat." Nora took the baby out of Chloe's arms. Howard was surprised at how little resistance Chloe showed at her mother's advances. He knew he had had more than enough of Nora the past few weeks and was ready for her to leave.

"Though, I was thinking it might be time to go home, and take Chloe and my grandbaby with me." Howard's shoulder pushed back as he jerked his head up at this. "You've been so kind," Nora continued, "taking care of our Chloe for us all these months, but she can't continue to expect you to take care of her, not now that she has a baby. That's too much to ask of anyone, much less a man that is ninety."

Howard looked at his granddaughter.

"Has she talked to you about this?"

"Grandpa, I don't know if I can take care of Mary on my own," Chloe started.

"Is this what you've been plotting, to take my granddaughter and great granddaughter away from me? I bet Meghan is in on this too." Howard confronted Nora.

"I did talk to Meghan. We are both concerned about your welfare. It's one thing to have a grown woman in your home, another to have a baby. You can't give Chloe the help she needs."

"And you can do that?"

"I am her mother."

"And you're okay with this?" Howard turned back to Chloe.

"I don't know, Grandpa. I can't raise a baby alone."

"You aren't alone. You've got me and all of our friends at the dance studio."

"But that's not the same as a husband."

"Plenty of women have raised children as single parents. What kind of nonsense has she put into your head?" Howard nodded at Nora.

Howard could see Chloe was struggling to know what to say. Her head was clouded by ebbing hormones. One minute she was elated at the small life in her arms, the next she was close to tears. The constant demand on her time, on her body, nursing the baby, changing diapers, sleepless nights. He remembered it all from his time with Helen, when her babies had been born. He remembered struggling to know how to help. But it was different now.

"And then there's your career," Nora spoke up. "You'll never be a star on Broadway with a baby to take care of."

"Is that what you want? To go back to New York?" Howard asked.

"I have thought about it, Grandpa. You know that."

"And I thought that had been decided when you didn't give up the baby for adoption."

"Nothing was decided, Grandpa. I just let it happen."

"And who better to raise a baby then her own flesh and blood," Nora said.

"Is that what you want? To let your parents raise your baby?"

"I don't know what I want."

"All the more reason to come home, regain your strength, work off that baby fat, and then you can decide about your career," Nora insisted

"Is that what you want? Because if it is, I can't stop you," Howard said.

"I don't know. I need to think."

"Will you, or will you just slip into a decision by not making a decision?" Howard had never spoken to her like that. He knew he was taking a chance but also knew he needed to speak up or risk losing both his granddaughter and great granddaughter. Chloe reached for her baby who was fussing in Nora's arms.

"I don't know, but what I do know is that Mary needs to be fed, so I will feed my baby. Not you, Mother, not you, Grandpa. I will do what only I can do." Chloe left the table. Nora and Howard looked at each other.

"Here, I'll clean the table." Nora stood up and began collecting plates. Howard followed after her into the kitchen. "I'm only doing what is best for the child," Nora told him.

"Are you? Are you doing what is best for Chloe, or are you doing what is best for Nora?"

"How can you say that? Why else would I take on a baby at my age?"

"So you can run her life the way you try to run everyone else's."

"No, because I won't let this baby ruin my daughter's life the way my daughter ruined mine." Nora's eyes blazed as she confronted Howard.

"Is that what you think, Mom? That I ruined your life?" Neither of them had noticed Chloe standing in the doorway of the kitchen. Nora and Howard exchanged glances as Nora fumbled for words.

"I didn't meant it, baby," Nora finally said.

"That explains it. I always knew I was a disappointment to you. Now I know why. I ruined your life. Well, don't worry, if my life is ruined, it's my own doing. I won't let Mary ruin your life too." Chloe walked out of the kitchen, Mary on her shoulder.

"What have you done now?" Howard asked her.

"I didn't know she was there. I only want what is best for her and my granddaughter."

"I'm not the person you need to tell this," Howard told her.

Chloe was nursing her baby when her mother knocked on her bedroom door.

"Stay out," Chloe said. Her mother opened the door.

"You couldn't keep me out when you were a kid. Do you think you can now?"

"What do you want? I've already ruined your life. Do you think I'm going to ruin Mary's life too?"

"No, I think you will be a wonderful mother. Better than I ever was, if that's what you want to do." Chloe continued to nurse Mary, focusing on the baby while her mother talked.

Her mother sat down on Chloe's bed. "You know, I was going to be the one on Broadway. I always had a flare for the dramatic, or at least that was what my mother always said, not in the most positive sense of the word, though. I wanted to have all the opportunities you had, dance lessons, acting classes, but we couldn't afford them."

"I know, Mom. You've told me this before."

"I had a chance though. I had that scholarship to attend that summer stock program in Vermont."

"I know. You told me about that too, so many times. It was the best summer of your life, but then you went home and got your nursing degree."

"It wasn't quite as simple as that. I met a young man at summer camp. I imagined I was in love. I came home from that summer internship with more than memories. I came home pregnant. I tried to hide the pregnancy from my parents, but, of course, I couldn't do that forever. They raised my baby as their own, but under the stipulation that I go to school and get a sensible degree. No more of this acting nonsense. At one point the plan had been that I would get a good paying job and raise the baby myself, but after the four years it took me to get my RN, and the time it took to get a good paying position, Jennifer had become such a part of my parents' life that there was no way to take her away from them. And then I met your father and that Catholic mother of his. I couldn't let her know about Jenny."

"Wait, are you telling me Aunt Jenny is actually my sister?" Chloe shook her head. "It can't be. Does she know?"

"No, and you better not tell her."

"I can't believe this. How could you keep this a secret all this time?" Chloe stood up, burping Mary on her shoulder and pacing about the room.

"It just happened. Times were different back then. It would have been a scandal. I never planned on it. I wanted to let Jennifer know, but then, the longer I waited, the more impossible it was to say anything." Her mother stood up and stopped Chloe from pacing. "So, you see, it wasn't you who ruined my life."

"No, it was my sister." Chloe was still struggling with the information. "But, Mom, you've been living a lie all those years."

"It's funny how the years slide by so quickly till you begin to believe the lie yourself." Her mother sat back down and looked at her lap. "Anyway, all my grand plans, all my dreams, all were gone. But then you came along. I decided to make sure you had everything I didn't have."

"Whether I wanted it or not."

"You took to dance like a natural. Was it that bad?"

"No, I guess not. I do love to dance."

"And you want to dance on Broadway, don't you?"

"I don't know any more, Mom. I'm confused. Here I thought I

was being my own person, living on my own in New York, only to find out I have a sister I never knew about and my dreams were not my own, but yours. That's a lot to take in at one time."

"You don't have to decide tonight. Give it some time. There is no time limit on the offer. We, your dad and I, would love to have you and our new granddaughter come live with us. What you do after that is entirely up to you."

"If only I could believe that," Chloe said.

"Yes, you can believe it. I promise." Chloe shifted Mary on her shoulder as she burped her.

One week later, Nora was on her way home without her daughter or granddaughter.

"The offer still stands," Nora said as she hugged her daughter goodbye. "Take care of my granddaughter," she added.

"I know and I will," Chloe assured her.

"Goodbye, old man," Nora extended her hand to Howard who pulled her close in a hug.

"Don't be a stranger. Come visit again, just not too soon," he said as he released her from his embrace.

Nora laughed. "That I will," she promised.

Howard and Chloe stood together and watched as she drove away until Mary began to fuss.

"Well, it's been an interesting few weeks," Howard commented. He didn't know what had passed between mother and daughter. Some things are best kept between the parties involved. He was just glad that Chloe was staying. He had gotten used to the company. The house would have been exceedingly empty without them. Now that school was over, Ashley was going to be coming over to help each afternoon.

"That it has been," Chloe agreed. "Mom sure has a gift for stirring things up."

"That she has." They walked together into the house.

Chapter 27

"So, are you going to have my great granddaughter baptized?" Howard brought up over dinner one night.

"I don't know. I guess I haven't thought that far. Grandma was Catholic, right? She brought my dad up Catholic, but he doesn't practice any more. I think I was baptized Catholic, but I don't know." They ate in silence for a while. Chloe slathered butter on her roll.

"Your grandmother loved butter," Howard said as Chloe slowly pulled the roll apart, relishing each bite.

"I know. Who do you think taught me to love butter."

"It was one of the things she missed the most during the war. Said she would never go without it again. She loved to drench her toast in butter."

"I hated it when you buttered my toast in the morning. You never put enough butter on it, not like Grandma." Chloe smiled. "I remember Grandma blessing me. Do you remember the blessings, Grandpa? What did she say?"

"I remember your grandma's blessings, but not the words. She used to do them in threes. I remember her dribbling three drops of water on our babies after they were born. She did it on you when she first saw you, when your mother wasn't around. Nora wouldn't have anything to do with your grandma's blessings. Said they were superstitious."

"I wish I knew what she said. I liked the blessings. She would make the sign of the cross on me at night and pray, sometimes in a strange language."

"That would be Gaelic."

"And when I left, she prayed over me, too. Sometimes it was in that other language, Gaelic, sometimes in English."

"She didn't speak Gaelic, at least not that I remember, but she said prayers in Gaelic. I remember her saying prayers in Gaelic even as she was forgetting everything else, who I was, your dad and aunt. They were the prayers from her childhood. Her grandmother had taught them to her." Howard paused as he remembered Helen crossing herself and speaking in Gaelic in the Alzheimer's unit. "And there was something about threes, three drops of water, three blessings to every prayer. It was connected to the Trinity."

"I wish I could bless Mary the way Grandma blessed me."

"Do you think you want to be talking to the priest?"

"I don't know. You're Presbyterian, aren't you, Grandpa?"

"Not a good one. I haven't gone to church since I left my parents' home."

"With all the fighting between the Protestants and the Catholics in Ireland, I'm surprised Grandma's family welcomed you into their home."

"They were Catholic, but they weren't closed-minded about other religions. Your great grandfather had fought in the war for independence from Britain, side by side with Protestants. I think that's where he learned tolerance. There were some, refused to fight for England in World War I or World War II. Insisted the Irish should only fight for the Irish, but not your mother's family.

"There were people who refused to associate with Protestants, Protestants who refused to associate with Catholics, but it wasn't everyone. It was a complicated situation, one I don't completely understand myself. The Protestants in Northern Ireland feared losing what they had if the Catholics had equal rights. The Catholics just wanted a fair shake in life. They wanted what everyone wanted. A home for their family and a job to put food on their table."

"The system was rigged against the Catholics?"

"Back then it was. I don't know about now." Howard shook his head. "So, do you think you might want to raise Mary as a Catholic? That was the one provision your grandma's parents insisted on before we marry, that our children be raised Catholic. The Catholic Church insisted or we wouldn't have been able to be married in the church."

"Did that matter?"

"Not to me, but to your grandmother and her parents it did. So I agreed."

"I wish I knew more. I just want Mary to feel blessed, the way I felt blessed when I visited you. I wish I had asked Grandma about it when I still could. It's too late now."

"Maybe not." Howard stood up.

"What are you talking about?" Howard went out of the kitchen then returned with a small, worn book.

"Your grandmother kept this book of prayers by her bedside for years. Perhaps it includes the prayers you remember. It appears to be written in Gaelic. Maybe you can find someone to translate it for you."

Chloe carefully picked up the worn book, afraid of it falling apart in her hands. In the margins she could see her grandmother's writing. "Thank you, Grandpa." She stood up and hugged him, all the while holding Mary in her arms. "Thank you," she said again, not knowing what else to say.

She looked again at the book. The words were a mystery to her, but it was a mystery she was determined to unlock.

Chapter 28

Northern Ireland, 1951

The reason Sean had been called away that night last year had been a false alarm, one of many it seemed. One day it would not be a false alarm. One day there would be real danger. Mary Helen dreaded that day.

"See, it weren't nothing."

"But someday it will be something. What do I do then?"

"You do what every good Irish Republican does. You fight for your country." Mary Helen didn't respond just as she didn't respond when Sean proposed marriage, putting him off.

"If you are looking for answers, you are looking in the wrong place," Granny surprised her one Friday morning. "Here, take the bus to St. Patrick's Purgatory. I've got your bag packed and I'll call work to tell them you are sick. When you get there, give this note to Fr. Timothy McCarthy." She handed Mary Helen the note and her bag.

"And you'll be needing this," she thrust her rosary into Mary Helen's hand and hustled her out the door.

"But what about breakfast?" Mary Helen tried to go back into the kitchen for a bite to eat.

"No, you're fasting."

"What?"

"No food. You can have some black tea, maybe a snug of sugar if you wish." With that, Granny pushed her out the door again. Mary Helen walked to the bus station and used the ticket Granny had given her. The return ticket was dated for Sunday. Three days gone, Mary Helen wondered to herself. That'll be an adventure. But she didn't know about this adventure. She had heard about St. Patrick's Purgatory, but not a lot. Granny didn't say much about it, but every year for as long as she could remember, Granny would be gone for three days to the Purgatory. She wondered why Granny wasn't coming with her.

Mary Helen checked her purse for money. She had enough to buy herself a decent Irish breakfast at one of the stops along the way, then thought better of it. Granny had gone to a deal of trouble to arrange this. She could at least try it out. At Lough Derg, she departed the bus and saw a boat waiting to transport her to the island. From the shore she could see buildings on the small island, including a large church and what appeared to be a monastery. The lake was smooth which made for an easy crossing.

She departed the boat with the other pilgrims and was met by a guide who instructed them to remove their shoes.

"The ground you are about to walk on is sacred ground, holy to Christians for centuries, ground that St. Patrick once walked on," he told them. Mary Helen pulled off her shoes then discretely unfastened her nylons to remove them and placed them in her shoes. Her bag and shoes were left in a storage area.

Mary Helen asked the guide about Fr. Timothy.

"He'll be available tomorrow morning," he told her.

"And what about meals?" she asked, regretting that she had missed her chance to eat breakfast or lunch before arriving.

"There'll be one meal today of dry toast and black tea. You may have it now or later this evening. Tomorrow you will have one meal as well. We are fasting while we are on the island," he informed the group. "There are nine prayer stations on the island. You will do one through three today at the Penitential Beds. Tonight you keep vigil in St Patrick's Basilica. You will have a rest period from 7:30-9:30p.m. before the vigil begins."

They were sent to begin their time of prayer. The Penitential Beds were all that remained of the beehive prayer cells that had once been used by monks as early as the ninth century. She walked and kneeled while praying simple prayers as instructed in the leaflet she had been given: 3 Paters, 3 Aves and the Creed. There was a rhythm and movement to the prayers that Mary Helen liked. It helped keep her thoughts at bay.

When rest time came, she couldn't rest as her mind kept buzzing and her stomach growled from lack of food. She was happy to have the vigil begin, with structured prayers, the Mass, Confessions and the Stations of the Cross. The movement and prayers helped keep her awake and focused. When left to her own devices, her mind wandered off to other matters and her head nodded.

The place was exceedingly quiet, even with the other pilgrims reciting their prayers. At first the quiet had seemed oppressive but as

Mary Helen relaxed into the rhythm of the place, it became a peaceful quiet. In her silent prayer time, Mary Helen found herself thinking about her grandmother. How long had she been coming here? What did she pray for when she was here? It was comforting to know she was walking ground her grandmother had walked before her. Then she found herself thinking about her life, where she had been, where she was headed. Her work at the shirt factory was far from fulfilling, but it was a job. Jobs were hard to come by, especially for Catholics. Some places boldly stated, "Catholics need not apply." Others were more subtle about their prejudice, asking where you went to school during the job interview; sending you on your way when you mentioned a Catholic school. Catholics and Protestants had their own schools, as separate as their churches.

Was that all there is to this life? Working at a mindless job until married and having children? What life did she have to look forward to here? There were so few opportunities for anyone, much less a Catholic woman. And what about Sean? What would life be like with him? Children, struggling to make ends meet, with a husband who might be gone at any time, off on IRA business or in prison. Was that what the future had in store for her? Sure, it was quiet now. There was no fighting going on, but that couldn't last.

As the night wore on, she found herself wondering about Howard. What was he doing? Surely by now he had married someone else, or had he? But what kind of life would she have with him, so far from her home and all she knew and loved. How could she leave? How could he have asked her? Maybe she hadn't loved him enough, not enough to leave.

Then she remembered Jimmy, how much she missed him. Why had he gone to war? Why hadn't he stayed and fought with the IRA like Sean? Then maybe he would still be alive. She had no answer to such questions. She was relieved to be up and walking a station to keep her body moving and her thoughts quiet.

The next morning she was brought to Fr. Timothy. She wondered if she could give him the note from Granny, and then, having discharged her duty, leave this island. Fr. Timothy was seated in a small room. The only furniture was two chairs and a small table between them with a Bible on it.

"What brings you here?" the priest asked as he stood up to welcome her and directed her to the extra chair. He was old, as Mary Helen had expected, but not as old as Granny, or at least he didn't appear to be as old as Granny.

Mary Helen handed him the note. "From my grandmother," was her only explanation.

Fr. Timothy unfolded the note, read it, then set it aside and looked at Mary Helen. "So, you are Veronica's granddaughter."

"Aye." Mary Helen squirmed under his firm gaze. She didn't know how, but with every priest she felt like she was back in Catholic school, waiting to be chastised for the least indiscretion.

"Did you read the note?" he inquired.

"No, Father. It wasn't addressed to me."

"How about we go for a walk. It's a beautiful day. We have to take advantage of it for we know it won't last." Mary Helen stood up as Fr. Timothy took her arm and tucked it into his, just like she were an old school chum.

"How long have you known my grandmother?" Mary Helen finally asked once they were far enough away from other visitors to not be overheard or disturb their prayer.

"It seems like just yesterday we were both kids, working on our fathers' farms, slipping off to play among the hills."

"You knew my granny as a child?"

"Grew up together. Our fathers were both farmers. Now she was the older of us two, but not by much by my reckoning, though, to your granny, it was a world of difference. She claimed to be boss because of the age difference."

"That sounds like Granny. I wonder why she never told me about you."

"Not much to tell. I went off to become a priest. She married and had children. She had always had an eye for my older brother. When he married Elise McDonald, she was heartbroken, tried to tell me she was going to be a nun. I told her no, she wasn't meant to be a nun, and sure enough, a year later she met your grandfather and the rest was history."

"How long has she been coming here?"

"For as long as I've been here. That's a good forty years."

"Tell me about Granny. What was she like when she was young?"

"She was always so full of life, that girl. She loved to have a good time. She never could understand why I became a monk and a priest. But God had a different plan for me than he had for her."

"I wonder if God has a plan for me."

"Of course he does. Why wouldn't he?"

"So you think it was God's plan that Granny marry and leave the farm?"

"Your grandmother had so much love to give. It was only natural that she fall in love and have children and grandchildren."

"But was that God's plan?"

"I think that's something you need to ask your grandmother. Only she can tell."

"And was it God's plan that her husband be killed in the war?"

"I don't know that all that killing was ever God's plan. We people, we seem to have plans of our own that don't go along with God's plan. But what about you? What are your plans? Surely you haven't come all this way just to talk about your grandmother."

"It wasn't my idea to come here. It was my Granny's."

"So how are you finding it so far?"

"I don't know. It's different than I had ever thought." They came to a bench that looked across the lake to the far shore. Fr. Timothy invited her to sit down.

"I like it here. I like looking across at the people on the shore, all going about their days with hardly a thought to us here on the island," the priest said.

"I don't think that's the case. How can they not be affected by being so close to this place?"

"Do you have a boyfriend?" Fr. Timothy directed the conversation back to Mary Helen, not letting her avoid talking about herself any more.

"Aye."

"Why so sad when you say that? Don't you love him?" Mary Helen hadn't realized that she had sounded sad.

"Aye, I do," she said, defending her relationship. "He asked me to marry him." Fr. Timothy just looked at her until she spoke again. "But how do I know what God wants me to do?"

"You don't. You just do it." This time it was Mary Helen's turn to look at him until he explained what he was hiding. "You never know for sure you're doing God's will. You do the best you can to live a good life and hope you are doing God's will." As Mary Helen continued to look confused he added. "You could start by asking him."

"But what if he doesn't answer or I get it wrong? It's not like he's writing to me in the sky."

"I see God in the sky, in the clouds, in the birds. I see God's presence everywhere."

"That's not what I mean. Were you this infuriating when you were a boy?"

"Worse. Just ask your grandmother." Fr. Timothy reached for her hand. "What if we ask God now?"

"You're wanting me to pray?"

"You do know how to pray, don't you?"

"Of course. I know all of the Catholic prayers, Pater, Ave, the rosary, the Creed. And Granny has been teaching me blessing prayers."

"But do you ever just talk to God?"

"Wouldn't that be wrong?"

"How could it be wrong? God loves it when we talk to him. Go ahead."

"Right now?"

"Right now."

"Out loud?"

"You can pray however you want. If you want to keep it just between you and God, do so."

"Okay," Mary Helen closed her eyes then opened them again. "Do I need to kneel down?"

"Only if you want to."

"Good," Mary Helen looked at the hard ground and decided to remain seated. "What should I say?" she whispered as she closed her eyes.

"Whatever is in your heart." Mary Helen fidgeted as she tried to make a beginning. The priest remained silent by her side. Finally, she began.

Dear God, she closed her eyes and bowed her head. *I don't know what to say.* She opened her eyes and looked to the priest for help.

"Why don't you ask God what his plan is for you?"

"Oh, right," Mary Helen bowed her head again.

Dear God, I don't know what your plan is for me, but whatever it is, I want to do it. Will you tell me? She waited but got no answer.

"God isn't answering." Mary Helen looked up again in frustration.

"Patience, child. God doesn't always talk the way we do. We have to listen with all of our self. We have to be silent and listen."

Mary Helen tried to listen, but patience wasn't her gift. "It's not working."

"It's not like magic where you say the right words and abracadabra, you get an answer. You have to wait and listen."

"I can't do this," Mary Helen stood up, ready to leave. Fr. Timothy took her hand and motioned for her to sit back down.

"Sometimes God doesn't speak to us in words but in images or feelings. When you try to pray, what image do you see?"

"I don't see anything," Mary Helen insisted.

"Try again. Close your eyes and wait and pray." Mary Helen closed her eyes, willing something, anything, to happen. Images, she thought to herself. What does God look like? She remembered pictures from her catechism, a grandfather figure in the clouds. She liked that. Was God like the grandfather she had never known, her grandma's husband? Then she thought about Granny. She wanted to cry. Granny was dying. She didn't want to admit it, but she knew it without saying the words. Granny was dying, she told the God in the clouds. Then she thought about Mary, the blessed Virgin, Holy Mother. It seemed she was comforting her. Then she asked, what is my future? What is your plan for me? She started to think about Sean, willing that to be the answer. She was surprised when Howard's face appeared in her head. She shook her head and opened her eyes.

"That can't be right," she stated.

"What did you see?" the priest asked.

"It doesn't make sense."

"What doesn't?"

"It has to be wrong?"

"Why do you say that?"

"Because when I asked God about his plan for me, the person whose face I saw wasn't my boyfriend."

"Who was it?"

"A soldier, an American G.I. I had met after the war. We had been engaged, but I couldn't leave Ireland so I broke it off with him. I've tried to put him out of my mind. Do you think I went against God's plan?"

"These things are never as clear as we imagine. It could, or it could mean that you have unfinished business with this soldier."

"It must be wrong. It's too late. I can't be with Howard, I'm with Sean now." Fr. Timothy waited patiently while she tried to sort it out. "God wouldn't want me to leave Ireland, would he, Father? Leave Granny, and Ma and Da?"

"Our history is full of people who did just that. St. Columba was forced to leave the country he loved, but in doing so brought the faith to parts of Europe that had been devastated during the Dark Ages. There's a long history of pilgrims. It's a matter of not getting 'stuck,' being willing to move on if that is what God is calling you too. We are all pilgrims in this world. Some are heart pilgrims — they aren't called to travel to faraway places, but their heart remains open to God, to moving on to new experiences, new relationships, wherever God is calling them to. It could be God is calling you to be a heart pilgrim, staying in your country but being open to God in new ways here, or perhaps God is calling you to leave, travel to new lands."

"But how do I know what God wants of me?"

"You don't. You just do the best you can."

"And if I get it wrong?"

"God will bless you anyway."

"What do you mean by that?" Mary Helen was getting impatient. This man was infuriating, even for a priest.

"Let's say that it was God's plan for a man to be a priest, but he chooses to marry instead. Does that mean he is forever out of God's grace?"

"I don't know." Mary Helen drew a line with her bare foot in the dirt below her.

"Some free will it would be if God condemned us every time we used it." Fr. Timothy paused to watch a bird fly by.

"I don't understand," Mary Helen looked up at him.

"I believe that God has a plan for us. God knows us better than we know ourselves and knows what will make us happy. We, however, don't always recognize what is in our best interest. Since we have free will, we are free to choose our own plans over God's plans for us. God won't condemn us or storm down fire and brimstone on us for doing this. He'll still bless us. But he won't rescue us from our poor decisions. We will still have to live out our lives, living with the choices we have made. Our life might be harder for having chosen our own path rather than the one God chose for us.

"In the case of the man who marries instead of becoming a priest, he may still have a good, full life, but he will struggle more than if he had chosen the path God had wanted. Does this make sense?"

"So, do you think God might want me to be a nun?"

"Do you want to be a nun?" Fr. Timothy's eyebrows rose.

"Heavens, no!" The priest laughed at this.

"Rest assured, I think I can say with some certainty that God is not calling you to be a nun. You are too much like your grandmother. But just because something seems impossible now, just because it would be hard, doesn't mean that is not what God is calling you to."

"But, it's too late. Howard is probably already married."

"And if so, then you have your answer."

"So you think I should try to find out?"

"I think you still have doubts about this man you say you are engaged to. I think it would only be fair to check out these doubts before you go ahead with marriage."

"Even if it means leaving Ireland?"

"Even if." Fr. Timothy stood up and looked at Mary Helen. "It seems you have a lot to think about and pray about."

"That I do."

"I hope the remainder of your time here goes well for you. Sometimes God's plans for us unfold over a long period of time. Have patience. I hope to see you again tomorrow before you leave." She stood up as well to give him a hug before he left. "Give my regards to your grandmother. Remember, it will become clearer over time. Be gentle with yourself," he said as he left. Mary Helen sat back down until called to the next station. She was relieved to get up and move. She tried to get her mind off of all that was whirling around inside her. After her light afternoon meal, her thoughts were more settled as she returned to the morning conversation.

"It will become clearer over time," she kept repeating to herself while trying to put her mind at ease. She was grateful for the structured prayers that helped keep her mind off of Sean and Howard. She was worn out from lack of sleep and food. Part of her couldn't wait to go home, resisted entering more fully into the retreat.

"And yet, this is how it must have been for St. Patrick those years he had served as a shepherd as a teenager," she told herself. Lack of sleep from watching over the flock, lack of food. The guide had shared Patrick's story, adding to what she remembered from her school days.

"It was said that Patrick was having a difficult time converting the Irish. We are a stubborn lot, as you know. So God led him to a cave. It was considered the gates to hell. There he showed Patrick the horrors of purgatory to let him know there is an afterlife. Pilgrims used to come and spend the night in vigil in the cave until the cave was closed off and St. Patrick's Basilica was built. Now we vigil in the church, staying up for twenty-four hours and fasting as way to help us hear God speak to us."

Mary Helen didn't know that she wanted God to speak to her. That morning had been enough. She wanted to go home, sleep in her bed and eat her Granny's cooking.

As she walked the stations she thought about what Fr. Timothy had said about God speaking in images. Unbidden, the image of her brother Jimmy came into her mind and she began to cry. It seemed the tears would not stop. Tears she had been holding back all of those years since his death; tears released by the discipline of hunger and no sleep. But as she cried, it seemed Jimmy was speaking to her.

"Everything's all right," he assured her. "I'm in a better place and someday you will see me again." Mary Helen continued to cry, but they were no longer tears of sadness, but tears of release, tears of joy. No one said a word to her as she cried. Tears were a familiar sight on the island. They were welcomed unlike the rest of the world where tears were treated as a sign of weakness.

She slept soundly that night, relieved from all of the grief she had held back, a sense of peace pervading her spirit.

She saw Fr. Timothy before leaving the island the next morning.

"Did you get the answer you sought?" he asked.

"No, but I will." Mary Helen said with confidence. "I got something better," she added. Fr. Timothy smiled. Standing before him was a different girl than had stood before him yesterday.

The feeling of peace remained with her throughout the long bus ride home. Even though she thought she would be starving after three days of fasting, she didn't eat the meal set before her that night when she got home but continued her fast of dry toast and black tea.

"I'll break my fast tomorrow morning," she told her mother. Granny nodded her head in agreement with her decision. Granny had been waiting for her when she got back.

"So, how was it? Did you talk to Fr. Timothy?"

"Aye, I did."

"And . . ."

"And nothing, Granny. I best be getting ready for bed. There's work to be done tomorrow," Mary Helen said, but she knew she hadn't fooled her grandmother.

Mary Helen knew what she was going to tell Sean, but she decided to take her time, not rush into anything. She kept repeating Fr. Timothy's words, "It will become clearer over time." What if she were wrong? Yet she knew she wasn't. Sean wasn't the one for her. She didn't know that Howard was the one for her either, but this much she knew.

Chapter 29

It was another whirlwind weekend for Letty, auditioning for the scholarship. This time Kevin wasn't in town but he had made arrangements with his roommate so Letty could stay in their apartment.

"You can stay with us all summer," Kevin told her. "I'll be gone most of the time so you can have my bed." But first she needed the scholarship. Auditions were a week before orientation for the summer session was to begin.

"Nothing like cutting it close," Letty complained to Chloe.

"How bad do you want this?"

"Real bad."

"Then you'll jump through the hoops."

"I guess I will." She would have stayed in New York that week. There certainly was plenty she could do while waiting for the summer session to begin. However that was the week of the dance camp at her church so she had to come back for that.

"Couldn't do it without you," Kathleen told her when she told Kathleen about going to New York.

Her parents had been skeptical when she told them her plans, but after thinking about it, they agreed to help her out with some of the expenses, paying for her flight for the audition and the $300 down payment on the class. Chloe hadn't booked a flight back to New York for the summer session. She wouldn't know until that week whether she had the scholarship or not.

The call came midweek, while at the dance camp. Letty left the class to take the call. Her face turned almost ashen as she hung up the phone.

"What is it?" Kathleen asked.

"I got the scholarship," Letty whispered.

"What?"

"I got the scholarship," Letty repeated, tears forming in the corner of her eyes. "I got the scholarship!" She laughed and broke out into a dance. The classes stopped as the instructors ran over to Letty to find out what was going on. The children followed after their teachers.

"Of course you got the scholarship," her mother pushed her way through the gathered students to hug her. Alicia had been helping with the dance camp, acting as a liaison for United Way. "I never doubted you."

Letty was hugging everyone when she stopped abruptly. "Wait, I've got to get tickets to New York."

"You mean these," Alicia waved an envelope in front of her face before handing it to Letty. "We didn't book a return flight in case you wanted to stay longer and sightsee. Besides, your father and I just might want to come out and see our daughter in the performance at the end of the summer."

"Mom, you did this? You bought me a ticket? But you didn't know I would get the scholarship?"

"I know this isn't exactly what your father and I had planned for our daughter, but if this is what you want to do, then we are behind you all the way." Letty hugged her mom.

"Really, Mom, you bought tickets before you even knew I would be going? What if I hadn't gotten the scholarship? You would have been out of the money. That doesn't sound like you."

"Well, your father and I discussed this as well. If you didn't get the scholarship money, we figured we could use what we had planned on spending on the remainder of your college tuition to pay for school. As it is, we can save that for if you ever do go back to school. And if for some reason you decided not to go to the summer session, what young girl wouldn't want a trip to New York? We doubted our money would be wasted."

"Mom, thank you. I don't know what to say."

"Just go to New York and make us proud."

"I'll do my best, Mom." Alicia hugged Letty again.

"My baby, dancing with the Alvin Ailey Dance Company," she said as she squeezed Letty.

"Mom, I'm not in the company. It's just a summer class." Letty pulled back from her mother.

"Not yet, but you will be."

Chapter 30

America, Summer 1951

Howard was surprised to receive a card from Belfast in familiar handwriting.

"What's this?" his mother asked. "I thought you had broken it off with that girl."

"It's nothing, Mom. Just a card. We're still friends." Howard brushed off his mother and went outside to read the card privately. It was a simple card with a picture of Belfast on the front.

Dear Howard,

I'm hoping this finds you well. We are well, though I'm doubting Granny is long for this world. She's been having trouble breathing. Something with her heart, the doctors say.

Give my regards to your family. If you have time, write me back. I would love to hear from you.

Sincerely yours,
Mary Helen Maguire

Now what was this about? Howard hadn't heard from Mary Helen since his visit two years ago. After all this time, why write now? It was as if she knew about his engagement. Howard hadn't asked Betty immediately after returning from Ireland. Having once been engaged and then breaking it off, he didn't want to go through that again. He wanted to be sure this time before proposing. First he had wanted both of them to have their degrees. Then they needed jobs, and money for a home of their own. So they had dated until Betty gave him an ultimatum.

"Howard, I've spent four years of my life on you. Other girls are married in much less time. How much time do you need to know I'm the one for you, because I'm not going to wait forever?" Howard stammered, trying to figure out what to say. "Is it still that Irish girl?" Betty asked.

"No, this has nothing to do with her. It's just that, I was wrong once. How do I know I won't be wrong again?"

That was not what Betty wanted to hear. Howard immediately regretted his words but couldn't take them back.

"I'm not getting any younger. All of my friends are already married and having babies. Either you propose to me, or we're breaking up."

"If you put it that way . . ." Howard paused. He didn't like being pushed into a corner. He didn't see any way out except through the door of matrimony.

"You do want to be married someday, don't you?" Betty asked.

"Yes."

"Okay, make up your mind. It's to me or I'm leaving."

Who else was he to marry if not her? His parents liked her, more importantly, his mother approved of her. She was everything he could ask for in a wife, smart, pretty, kind.

"Betty," he started, "will you . . ."

"Get down on one knee," Betty demanded. "I want a real proposal, not a half-hearted one."

Howard did as she asked, proposed and Betty accepted. "Now was that so bad?" she said as she helped him off his knee and kissed him. It hadn't been her idea of the perfect proposal, but it had been a proposal. "Now we have to buy the ring," she instructed her suitor.

Howard smiled and kissed her back. "No, it wasn't so bad at all," he said, kissing her again.

"Grandpa, you didn't really propose like that!" Chloe interrupted Howard's narrative.

"What was wrong with it?"

"It's not exactly romantic."

"Things were different back then from today. Not so much hoopla around the proposal or the wedding. It was enough to have a ring and say the words. I feel sorry for young men today. So much pressure to do something spectacular."

"When I get married, I want the proposal to be special, like maybe during a trip to Cancun, or Paris, some place romantic."

"That's what we used to call a honeymoon."

"Whatever, Grandpa. Go on. I'm sorry I interrupted."

"After that, all we needed was the wedding. I was all for a quick and simple ceremony, but not Betty. She wanted a big church wedding with attendants and a proper reception afterwards. Nothing like what's expected today, but more than a justice of the peace and a ten-minute ceremony, like Sheila and George did. It was lucky for me that Betty took her time."

"Why was that?"

"Because it gave me time to back out."

"Is that what you did?"

"Let me tell the story."

The wedding had only been a few weeks away when Howard received the card from Mary Helen. He had thought he had pushed her out of his head, but here she was again. Perhaps it was cold feet. He showed Betty the card.

Betty read it then gave it back to him. "What does this have to do with anything?" she asked.

"I just thought you should know. I mean, since we are getting married, I didn't want to be keeping any secrets from you . . ." Howard fumbled for words.

"Is this your way of getting out of the marriage?"

"No, of course not. That was the past. You are my future."

"Then tear it up." Betty handed the card back to him.

"What?"

"You heard me, tear it up. If this Mary Helen means nothing to you, then tear up the card."

"She's still a friend," Howard protested.

"An ex-girlfriend." Betty crossed her arms on her chest. Howard knew there would be no budging her. He tore the card in two.

"There, satisfied?"

"Yes, I am." Betty smiled and kissed him. "I'm not sharing you with anyone." Howard kissed her back, but tucked the torn card into his back pocket.

"Have you made arrangements to have your suit pressed for the wedding?" Betty launched into wedding plans. Howard fingered the torn card while Betty chattered away.

The next morning he checked on flights to Ireland. He booked one for that night, packed a bag and made arrangements to be off work for a few days. He sent a message to Betty that he had been called out of town for work. "I'll explain when I get back," he wrote in the message. He had gone out of town on business before so Betty wasn't entirely surprised. As a mechanical engineer he needed to work on different buildings throughout the state.

He arrived in Dublin at five their time, took a bus to Belfast, all the while wondering what he was doing. What would he say when he saw Mary Helen? What would she say to him? What if she were married? So foolish of him to travel this far without writing back to her first. But if he had done that, he may not have heard back from her before the wedding. No, better this way. If she were married, he would have his answer and would leave and not look back. And if she were not married . . . he would deal with that then. Perhaps he was making the biggest mistake of his life, coming all of this way on a whim. Betty was a great gal. He didn't want to lose her. But then what was he doing here?

"Betty need never know," he told himself. "I'll see Mary Helen one more time then come home." He got a room in a downtown hotel, avoiding the one where Mary Helen's father worked. He didn't want anyone to let Mary Helen know he was there. He wanted to surprise her. Hopefully it would be a good surprise. He went to his room, showered then laid down to catch up on his lost sleep but couldn't sleep. He figured Mary Helen was at work and wouldn't be available until that evening. Rather than pacing to and fro in his room he decided to walk about the city and get something to eat.

He walked to some of the places he had visited with Mary Helen on that first date when she and Brigid had showed him and his buddies the city. It wasn't the same as being with her, and yet it was strangely similar. He felt her presence. From the moment of landing on Irish soil, she felt near to him. Her spirit permeated the streets of Belfast. Memories came flooding back, taking him back to a time when he had been younger, back before Ronnie's death and George's injuries. Back to a simpler time in war torn Belfast.

He remembered the announcement that the war was over. He remembered the excitement throughout the streets as people paraded and cheered. And he remembered a young girl dancing an Irish jig. There were no remaining remnants of the war, at least that he could see. Time had healed the broken buildings even if not the spirits broken by the war. Despite the war, or maybe because of it, it had been a more innocent time. The allies had won, the Nazi German threat overcome and he had been happy and in love. Everything had seemed possible back then.

But that had been then. The world did not know the extreme atrocities of the Nazi prisoner of war camps or the carnage of the atomic bomb. That had only come to light months after the war had been over. It had been a simpler time.

After lunch Howard went back to his room and waited for quitting time at the shirt factory where Mary Helen worked. He caught the bus there, arriving an hour ahead of time. He walked the streets, smoking a cigarette to help pass the time. He saw groups of women leaving the building. Finally he saw Mary Helen walking with her arms linked with two friends, laughing and talking, just as he remembered her. He threw the cigarette down and approached the trio.

"Mary Helen?" He didn't dare smile, not till she smiled and let him know he was welcome. The trio stopped as Mary Helen stared at the American blocking their way.

"Howard?"

"Yes, it's me."

"Is this your American GI? The one you used to talk about?" One of her friends nudged her and laughed.

"Aye, I believe tis." Mary Helen addressed Howard, "What are you doing here?"

"You said to write."

"That I did."

"Well, I'm not much of a writer."

"That I know." Mary Helen was still standing with her arms linked with her friends.

"Can we talk?" Howard asked. "Maybe get dinner?"

"Aye." Mary Helen let go of her friend's arms. "Brenda, tell me mum I won't be home for supper." Howard held out his arm and she linked her arm in his as they walked.

They took the bus downtown to a restaurant they had frequented back after the war. After dinner they walked along the locks.

"Isn't this where they built the Titanic?" Howard, the engineer, was always interested in boats and construction.

"We don't like to talk about that. The unsinkable boat that sank. Not exactly our best. Tis an embarrassment." They walked in silence for a while.

"It's so good to see you again," Howard said for the third time that evening.

"And good it is to see you," Mary Helen repeated her response. "But what brings you to Belfast? The truth now."

"Your note."

"It was just a note."

"Was it?"

"Aye." Mary Helen looked at him for a moment then turned away, refusing to meet his gaze.

"I thought it was something more."

"What more could it be?"

"I thought, maybe, maybe you had second thoughts about me, about us?"

"You thought that, just from a note?"

"Yes, I did. Was I wrong? The truth, no lies between old friends." Howard stopped walking and faced her, trying to see her face in the dimming light.

"Nay, you weren't wrong." Mary Helen turned away from him and continued to walk.

"Does that mean, there's still hope for us?" Howard stopped her, taking her hand and again looking into her face.

"Aye." Mary Helen responded softly, her eyes cast down. "I'm thinking, that is, if you'll still have me."

Howard put his hand to her chin and raised her eyes to his and gently gave her a kiss in response.

Chapter 31

With her mother gone, Chloe welcomed Ashley's help with Mary. Ashley rode her bike over to her grandfather's several days a week, when the weather allowed. With school out, Ava was available to help watch Jacob and Grace during the week, giving both grandmas a break. Ashley insisted she didn't need watching and would take off on her bike to Howard's where she helped Chloe with Mary. With the competitions scheduled over the summer and into the fall, Ashley wasn't able to take the summer off from dance practice. Chloe fixed a place in the basement for Ashley to practice. Somedays Kathleen came over to check on Ashley's progress as well as Chloe's progress.

"You are going to teach for us this fall, aren't you?" Kathleen asked over lunch.

"I haven't figured out childcare for Mary yet."

"Bring her with you. That's what Joy used to do when the kids were little. There are always plenty of mom's around willing to help out."

"And then there's the trip we are planning to Ireland."

"We can work around that."

"And eventually I'll need a job where I can work more hours and make more money."

"I don't know what I can do about that just yet. I'll do what I can." Kathleen leaned back and thought. "You can teach the Irish step dance class under Patrick's supervision." In order to compete, teachers had to be associated with a certified school of dance. Kathleen had already worked this out with Patrick. Chloe would teach the beginner classes. Students who progressed beyond that would go to his studio in Plymouth. In this way, Joy's Dance Studio would be a feeder for his school, allowing him to reach more students without having to be on the road as much.

"I'll think about it."

"And you can help Letty with the other classes." Chloe didn't say anything about this. She had been talking to Letty while she was away and knew she was considering a move to New York. It wasn't her place to say anything. That was for Letty to do.

"There now. There's no reason for you to be thinking about moving or looking for another job." Her grandfather entered the conversation. "You can stay here for as long as you like. I can help with Mary Helen. You don't need a lot of money."

"Grandpa, I can't impose on you forever." Chloe appreciated the offer, but was worried about leaving Mary with her grandfather. Even though he was in good health for his age, there still was the matter of age. She was afraid he might not be up to it.

"It's no imposition, you know that. I love having you and Mary Helen here," Her grandfather insisted. They had been over this before.

"So what's happening with you and Pastor Joe?" Her grandfather asked Kathleen. Kathleen squirmed.

"Nothing. It's over. Over before it ever began."

"That's not what I thought. You two seemed good together."

"Seemed is the operative word. We are too different. Me, with a minister? Not happening."

"But why?" Howard asked. Chloe could tell Kathleen didn't like this line of questioning. Howard continued, "Some would say, Helen and me, we were too different. She wanted excitement. She was always full of life, whereas I was kind of a stick in the mud, staid, predictable. I think it was the differences that kept our marriage interesting. On the important things, like family, we agreed."

"Well, what might work for you, won't necessarily work for everyone," Kathleen said.

"Maybe not."

"How did we go from Chloe to me?" Kathleen asked.

"Welcome to my world," Chloe smiled. "I don't know, Grandpa, you aren't always predictable."

"If not, it's not because of me. It's because of Helen's influence."

"Maybe so, Grandpa, but that's not how I see it." Chloe excused herself to nurse Mary.

When Michelle found out that Chloe was helping Ashley prepare for competitions this summer, she called and asked if Chloe would take her on as well.

"I'll pay you. I've got my babysitting money." At first Chloe was unsure about taking on any students, but as word got out that she was available, other members of Ashley's dance class asked for help as well. She was able to give them private lessons in her grandfather's basement while Ashley helped with Mary.

"Maybe we should consider summer classes," Kathleen said to Chloe when she heard about the students. Chloe knew Kathleen didn't like having the dance studio closed all summer, but she didn't have the teachers or the students. Most of her students were busy with other activities over the summer, their parents happy to be free of the strain on their budgets and schedules. Letty had suggested they do another dance camp for low-income children as they did each spring break and so they had set this up for June at Letty's church so they didn't incur any costs for air conditioning the studio. After that her teachers, including Letty, were gone for the summer. Holding summer classes would mean the added expense of air conditioning, and other expenses. Kathleen had talked to Chloe about it at length over the summer.

Why did she feel she was being lured into something . . .?

Chapter 32

Northern Ireland, 1951-52

Howard flew back to Michigan a few days after that night at the Belfast locks. He and Mary Helen made plans that she would book voyage on a boat to New York as soon as she was able. But first, he had to break it off with Betty.

"I suspected all along that you weren't over that Irish girl." Betty hadn't taken it well. She threw her engagement ring at him. "Here, give this to your Irish girl. If you change your mind again, don't be looking for me."

His discomfort over the breakup didn't last long. There was no doubt in Howard's mind that Mary Helen was the one for him. Even though Mary Helen and Howard had agreed that she would come to America as soon as she could, it was left to Mary Helen to determine how soon that would be.

"I can't leave my Granny just yet," she told him. Howard accepted this, knowing this time that it was just a temporary delay.

"I've waited this long, what's a few months more?" he told her.

"Now don't you be a staying because of me," Granny told Mary Helen when she said she didn't know when she would be going to America.

"And why would I? You're just another person wanting to be taken care of as far as I can see, even with your stories. Besides I've heard them all. If I stay, it's because I choose to stay for now."

"Stubborn young folk, always think they know best," Granny muttered.

"And if I am stubborn, who do I have to blame for it?"

It was no surprise when Granny took to her bed again that winter, struggling to breathe. They propped her up with as many pillows as they could find to help relieve her congestion and make it possible for her to sleep. Da wanted her to go to the hospital, but Granny refused.

"If I'm to die, let me do so in me own bed," she told him.

"Now don't you be talking of dying, old woman," Ma chided her. "We've had enough of death here. You have plenty of life left in you."

"That woman's too stubborn to die," Granda Mike commented. He took to his pints, refusing to acknowledge the specter that hung over the house. "Tis I should be dying, not her," he stated as he drank. Granny was the younger of the two and had always been more active.

"Perhaps it's because you are preserved by all the alcohol you drink, old man," Liam said as he joined him in a draught.

Death comes in its own time. After a month of struggling to breathe, Granny drowned in the fluid built-up in her chest as she was no longer able to cough the phlegm free from her throat. It seemed a blessing to her family that she was out of her suffering, yet it came too soon. Death always comes too soon to our loved ones. Death took its time, came slowly, but it was still too soon.

They waked her in the living room, then buried her the next day after the funeral Mass. Sean came to the wake with his family. When he saw Mary Helen slip outside for some fresh air, he followed her out.

"It's sorry I am, for your loss."

"No more sorry than I am. She was more than a grandmother to me."

"I hear you'll be going to the States."

"Aye, when it can be arranged. Now that Granny is gone there is nothing holding me here."

"You won't miss the old country?"

"I'll miss it and the people, but there will be new people to meet and new opportunities for me."

"And will you miss me?"

Mary Helen refused to look at him as he asked, turning away and staring off into the dark. He took her by the shoulders, turned her around with his strong arms and forced her to look him in his eyes. "Ah, my Mary Helen, why are you running away from your country, your home, from me?" he said as he kissed her full on the lips.

Mary Helen allowed the kiss for a moment then pulled away. "I'm not running from, I'm running to, running to a new life."

"But why? Why can't you make your life here?"

"I'll not be wife to a dead man."

"I'm far from dead. I'm here and I love you, isn't that enough?"

"You may be here now, but you won't be. You'll be going off to fight, if not today, or the next day, then someday. I don't want to stay around to see the people I love be killed by hatred. Not just you, but your brother, my sister's husband, and my brother."

"Is that it? Is it just my involvement with the IRA? I'll give it up."

"You know you won't, and I won't ask you. Don't be lying to me Sean O'Connor. I've known you too long. You were born to fight. It's your nature. If you gave it up you would come to resent me for it. You would go back to it after a while. But it's not my nature to sit at home and tend the hearth fire waiting for you."

"Don't you love me? Don't you love Ireland?"

"Aye, I do love you and my country."

"Then why are you leaving?"

"Because, I love another more. It's taken me some time to realize it, but I'm meant to leave this country and follow that man."

"Then, if that's the case, I'll not stand in your way."

"I do love you." Mary Helen reached up and kissed him. She couldn't resist one last kiss. "But I love another."

"Then I'll be wishing you well and be on my way," Sean said, slipping down the street without returning inside to make his goodbyes. Mary Helen rejoined the group toasting Granny and sharing memories of her life.

Mary Helen had tried to reach Fr. Timothy to let him know about Granny's death. When she wasn't able to reach him by phone, she sent him a letter. Fr. Timothy wrote back and included the note Granny had sent with her to him when she had gone on retreat last year.

My dear Timmy,

I'm sending you my granddaughter, Mary Helen, for your guidance. She doesn't realize it but she is struggling to know God and God's plan for her life.

I'm not long for this world and when I go she will need a friend. I hope you can be that friend for her, or at least point her on her way as you've done for me so many times.

And so, my little brother in Christ, I take my leave of you, entrusting my precious granddaughter to your care. May our blessed Mother and all the Saints watch over and guide you and her.

Your Sister in Christ,
Rona Maguire

Tears choked Mary Helen's throat as she read and reread the letter. She crinkled the paper into a ball as she cried, her hands collapsing into fists. She wanted to hit someone, anyone, but there was no one there. She dropped the wad of paper and covered her face with her hands as the tears flowed, then, realizing what she had done, she sought out the letter and smoothed it out, trying not to let any drops of tears mar its surface.

Mary Helen had suspected that the note was about her when she had delivered it; still it seemed her grandmother was reaching from beyond the grave to speak to her. She brought the letter to her lips to kiss, a concrete reminder of her grandmother. Something physical she could kiss now that her grandmother's body was no longer among them.

She wondered about her grandmother's relationship with Fr. Timothy. She had asked her about it one time last summer, after her retreat. Granny had said he was her soul friend.

"What's a soul friend?"

"Everybody needs a soul friend."

"But what is it?"

"Someone you can talk to about what's important in this life and the next. Not just everyday conversation, but real conversation, heart talk," Granny reached over and touched her on her chest. Mary Helen wrapped her arms around her chest in an embrace, remembering how Granny had touched her heart.

"Then that's what you are for me, a soul friend."

"Am I now?" Granny had smiled and took a pull from her pipe.

Chapter 33

Since getting the Gaelic prayer book from her grandfather, Chloe had been fascinated with the language and everything Irish. She researched it on the internet and found a website for learning Gaelic. She also went to the library and was able to get books on Gaelic through the inter-library loan system. It helped to pass the time when she was nursing Mary or rocking her to sleep, or just holding her. Chloe had become quite adept at holding her baby in one arm and holding a book in the other. She had a wraparound sling that she could put the baby in and carry on her chest. As Mary got bigger she would eventually be able to carry her on her back, like a papoose.

While she hadn't completely resigned herself to staying in Cascade Falls, it was a good enough place for now. She definitely did not want to move back in with her parents and New York was out of the question until Mary was older, if ever. Cascade Falls wasn't so bad for the time being.

She packed Mary in her car seat in the backseat of Howard's car and drove to the library. Howard had offered to watch Mary while she went.

"No, Grandpa. I need to get used to going places on my own with Mary. We won't be gone long," she had told him. He laid down for a nap while they were gone.

She scanned books in the library, Mary quietly sleeping in her wrap, until the baby started to fuss. Chloe was on her way home when she heard a pop. The car started to thump. She pulled over to the side of the road, got out and found one of the tires was flat.

"What do I do now?" Chloe asked herself. She couldn't call her grandfather. Even if he heard the phone and answered, what could he do? He didn't have a way to get there and help her. Did he have road service? Chloe looked through the glove compartment. She found Howard's registration and proof of insurance, but didn't see a number to call for road service.

Mary started fussing in the backseat. Even with the windows down, it was way too hot inside the car so Chloe unbuckled the car seat, pulled it out and looked for some shade for her baby. Just then she heard the short bleep of a siren. A police car pulled up behind her.

"Do you need any assistance?" the police officer approached.

"Yes, I've got a flat tire."

"Is there anyone I can call for you?"

"No, or, I don't know. My grandfather, but he can't help."

"Whose car is this?"

"My grandfather's." Chloe handed him the registration and insurance from the glove compartment.

"Does he have road service?"

"I don't know. I guess I can try calling his insurance company."

"It looks like you have your hands full," the officer indicated the baby. "I'll call the local auto shop and see if they can send someone out to help."

"Thank you," Chloe pulled Mary out of the hot car seat and gently bounced her to calm her down.

"They're sending someone right over. It won't take long to switch out the tire. Do you have a spare?"

"I guess so. I never checked." The officer popped open the trunk and pulled out the spare.

"He'll either bill your insurance or you can pay him and be reimbursed."

"Okay, officer, thank you," Chloe continued to bounce Mary.

"It's Officer Nash," he introduced himself. "I don't believe we've met."

"I'm Chloe Jones. I'm staying with my grandfather, Howard Jones."

"He helps out at the arts center downtown, doesn't he?"

"Yes, he does. Do you know him?"

"I believe so. I know the family that runs the center, the Reese family."

"Yes, Kathleen Reese. I teach dance classes there."

"I know her, her sons and her mother and her stepfather."

"That might not be a good thing," Chloe joked. "It depends on how you know them."

Officer Nash laughed. He continued to chat with her and didn't leave once the tow truck arrived and the mechanic fixed the flat tire.

Chloe had been put off at first by the arrival of the officer. She had not had many interactions with the police, except for that one time she was stopped during high school because of her tail light being out.

She had been too focused on Mary at first to pay attention to him, but as he called for assistance, she glanced at him and noticed his angular brown face and muscular body. He pulled his hat off as he spoke and ran his hand through his short cropped hair then placed it back on. She checked for a ring on his finger. Nothing.

The mechanic was finishing up as Officer Nash received a call.

"I've got to go." He reached out his hand. "It was a pleasure to meet you, Ms. Jones."

"Chloe," Chloe corrected him as he wrapped her hand in a firm grip.

"Chloe," He released her hand. "Maybe I'll see you again some time," he said, tipping his hat as he left.

"Maybe," Chloe said. She was still staring in his direction when interrupted by the mechanic with paperwork for her to sign. "Maybe," Chloe repeated as she sat in the driver's seat and prepared to drive home.

Chapter 34

The six weeks had been the most strenuous in her life. Letty had thought she was in good shape, but not like this. Eight hours a day of practice, five days a week and sometimes on the weekends as well. They were definitely testing whether she had it in her to be a professional dancer. How could she ever have thought she was ready to audition for the main company? Even with all of her training, all of the classes she had attended and taught, it was nothing like she was experiencing now.

Living in New York was an education in itself, even with the limited time she had to see the sights and experience the city. She hopped on the subway each morning, trying not to be too obvious about observing all the people around her. So many people from so many different cultures, African American, Asian, white, Hispanic, young, old and every age in between. Some in rags, others fashionably dressed. Some with ear plugs, heads nodding along to music only they could hear. She stepped over street people and listened to street performers on her way to the dance studio from the subway at Columbia Circle. She had suspected that her life in Cascade Falls was a constricting cocoon, a warm safe place her parents had created to protect their baby girl from the "real" world, she just didn't realize how limited her experiences had been until living in New York. She hoped it wasn't too obvious as she walked the streets of the theater district, gazing in awe at Carnegie Hall, Times Square, and the multitude of buildings, old and modern constructions, that made up New York.

On the weekend, when she had time off, she visited the 9/11 Memorial on the site of the former twin towers of the World Trade Center. Even amidst the crowds, she felt a sense of awe, as if in a church sanctuary. She felt the presence of the thousands of lives lost. She felt a sense of peace as she sat there and said a prayer before moving back into the masses and noise of the city.

She also enjoyed looking at the Statue of Liberty, wondering about the many refugees that had sought asylum through this harbor. She recognized her own ancestors had come on slave ships from Africa, probably in some southern harbor, not under this beacon of hope. Still she appreciated the statue and all it represented. It was through this harbor that so many of the different ethnic groups that made up the New York she was learning to love had come.

From the harbor, she took the subway to Central Park where she could wander for hours, eat cheap from an outside vendor, and enjoy the day without spending the fortune she did not have.

But most of all, she loved the Alvin Ailey Studio, the floor to ceiling windows in the classrooms, the high ceilings. It was like another sanctuary. At times she would come early or stay late in order to have time on her own in the classroom to stretch and work on her moves. She wanted to make as much as she could out of this summer, regardless of what happened afterwards.

Each summer they had a guest choreographer. She had auditioned to be in her class and made it. She was determined to justify the faith others had shown in her: her parents, Chloe, Kathleen and the people at Alvin Ailey who had given her the scholarship.

When the six weeks were drawing to a close with no invitation to audition for Ailey II, Letty resigned herself to coming home and another year at the dance studio. She was going to stay an extra week to sightsee before going back. Her parents had come for the performance and were staying for a few days as well. She was looking forward to seeing them but feeling a bit like she had let them down.

"What are you talking about?" her dad asked at dinner the night they got into New York.

"You were thinking I would be dancing with the Alvin Ailey Dance Company someday."

"You are dancing for Alvin Ailey. That's all we could wish for," her mother said. "Then afterwards you can come home, put this behind you and get on with your life."

"I guess." Maybe it wasn't them she had let down, but herself. She was surprised at how disappointed she had been to not get an invitation to audition, but put it aside the next day in order to focus on the performance.

The performance went well. They were greeted with loud applause. Letty liked the sound. Better not get used to it, she told herself as this was to be her one and only performance in New York. She was happy about her performance in the show, but sad at the end of the summer session. As one of her instructors hugged her, she handed her an envelope with a card in it.

"What's this?" Letty asked.

"Your invitation to audition for Ailey II. We have an opening for the fall." She left Letty standing in shock, the envelope unopened in her hand. Alicia and Cliff found her there, still holding the envelope.

"What's that?" her mother inquired.

"An invitation to audition."

"That's great, baby," her father hugged her. "You're as good as in."

"Let's see it," her mother took the envelope out of her hand and pulled out the card. "It sure 'nough is the real thing." Her mother kissed the card before giving it back to Letty.

"Don't say that. First I have to audition, then I have to get in and then, after two years, I may get into the dance company, but I may not."

"You'll get in," Alicia confirmed what Cliff had said. "And if not, you can always come home."

Letty said goodbye to the friends she had made over the summer.

"Letty, I'm so excited for you, and jealous," each said in their own way when she told them the news. "Of course you'll get in. You have to. I can't wait to see you dance on Broadway someday."

They were more confident than she was. Then it occurred to her, "How do I tell Kathleen?"

Chapter 35

Northern Ireland - Spring 1952

Mary Helen had never been on a plane and wasn't ready to start so she waited till spring to book passage on a liner. It was hard saying goodbye to her family, especially not knowing when she would see them again. She said goodbye to her Ma and Granda Mike at home, hugging them tight. Her father and Brigid went with her to the boat dock, Brigid toting her 2 year old and another on the way. Mary Helen caught a glimpse of Sean at work before boarding. She started to wave but he didn't see her. Brenda, her friend from work was joining her so she didn't have to travel alone and had someone to share a cabin with. They leaned over the railing, waving at their families as the boat pulled away.

The trip was long and uneventful, long enough to help Mary Helen make the transition from Ireland to a new country. When she saw the Statue of Liberty in the New York harbor, she felt she was coming home. She stood on the deck, gazing at the statue.

"She's more beautiful than I imagined," she said to Brenda who was standing next to her.

"That she is."

Travelling with her were all the letters she had received from Howard over the years and the note her grandmother had sent to Fr. Timothy, along with a book of blessings in Gaelic, lest she forget the old ways.

"Don't forget our traditions, there in America," Granny had told her. Some of the last words to come out of her mouth before she was no longer able to speak.

"I won't, Granny," she said as the boat pulled into dock at Ellis Island.

Howard had planned to meet her in New York, but Mary Helen said no.

"I want to see America by myself first to get me own impression of the country," she had written him. "I'll be safe. I'll be travelling with Brenda and staying with cousins in New York. They'll help me catch the train to Detroit."

When asked her name for entry into the United States, she stated, "Helen Maguire."

"But your name is Mary Helen," Brenda confronted her afterwards.

"I'm leaving Ireland behind and accepting America as my new home. I'm no longer Mary Helen, but Helen, and soon I'll be Helen Jones, a true American," Helen told her.

"So that's why she went by Helen, not Mary Helen," Chloe said as Howard finished his story.

"Yes, she studied to be an American citizen and never looked back. Helen remained true to her promise to make America her home. She embraced the customs of the country, like the Fourth of July and Thanksgiving, as her own. She also kept her promise to her grandmother in her own way. She prayed her prayers of blessing, but when her children, your father and aunt, showed no interest in learning about the old ways, she didn't insist. Her children were brought up Catholic, as she had promised her parents and the church, but as adults, they went their own way."

"She never looked back?"

"Well, almost never. She did visit her home from time to time, getting over her fear of flying in order to go home in a day. And her parents came to visit once."

"And what about Sean O'Connor?"

"He continued in the IRA. He came to visit once when in America. We suspect he was buying guns, but we didn't ask him about it."

"What was he like then?"

"Older. Harder than when I last saw him in Belfast, still a charmer."

"Oh?"

"But his charms no longer worked on my Helen."

"How do you know that?"

"Because she told me so. She said it was good to see him, but she knew he was involved in all the violence during the 70's. He ended up in prison again, took part in the resistance in prison. He knew Bobbie Sands and the other hunger strikers."

"Who is Bobbie Sands?"

"What do they teach you in school? You best be learning your history, especially if you want to be going to Northern Ireland with me."

"Okay, so tell me."

"He was the first of the hunger strikers to die. Margaret Thatcher wasn't about to give in to their demands. It was an international incident. Look it up."

"But what happened to Sean?"

"He died shortly after he got out of prison in a bombing mishap. The bomb exploded in transport."

"Oh," Chloe took some time to grasp what he had said. "And what about Grandma's brother Liam?"

"He immigrated to Australia when it became clear he was no longer safe in Ireland. He died in the '90s but has family there still."

"Are any of Grandma's family still in Ireland?"

"Her sister Brigid is still alive, but that's it for her immediate family. But there are plenty of cousins for you to meet."

"That's good," Chloe frowned as she thought. "Do you think Grandma ever regretted leaving Ireland?"

"If she did, she never showed it to me. Later, when the Alzheimer's progressed, she used to speak in Gaelic. It was like she was returning to the old country in her mind."

Chloe was sad to have the story over. "What will we talk about now?" she asked.

"There's plenty to talk about young woman, like plans for your baby girl and plans for our trip to Ireland."

They were planning on going in the fall, after the main tourist season was over.

"It'll be easier to travel when there are fewer tourists on the road and easier to get accommodations," Howard instructed.

Chloe's dad was making the trip with them. "At his age, it's pretty risky for your grandfather to be travelling so far."

"He says he'll be okay." Chloe was worried about it as well.

"That's all right. I'll come along with you. I always wanted to see Ireland. My mother used to talk so much about it."

"What about Mom? Is she going to come?"

"Didn't she tell you? She has a new job. She quit her position as head nurse at the retirement community and is now Activity Director.

It was a cut in pay, but she loves it. She has the residents putting on musicals and shows. I've never seen her happier. She can't leave because they will be in the middle of a production of 'Fiddler on the Roof' when we go."

Chloe laughed. She was relieved to know she would not be contending with her mother during the trip.

"You'll be back in time for the National Competition in Chicago, won't you?" Ashley asked Chloe when she learned about the trip.

"Wouldn't miss it." At one point Ashley had hoped to go as well.

"You're in training," Chloe reminded her. "Besides, if you qualify for the International Competition you'll be going to Dublin next year."

"But will Uncle Howard be able to come?"

"I'll be there," Howard told her. "Lord willing and the crick don't run dry," Howard told her.

"What does that mean?" Ashley asked.

"It means he'll be there," Chloe told her.

Chapter 36

"You've been so good to me over the past few years, encouraging me, even paying for those dance classes in Detroit," Letty started.

"Are you telling me you're leaving?" Kathleen interrupted her prepared speech. Letty was flustered. Finally she responded.

"Yes, I've been accepted to be part of Ailey II, part of the Alvin Ailey Dance School. It's like a two-year internship." Letty had expected Kathleen to be more upset.

"It's not like I didn't see this coming. I knew it was a possibility when you went to New York this summer. Who wants to stay in Cascade Falls once they've been to New York? I know I wouldn't."

"But I don't want to leave you in a bind. Maybe I could postpone starting until you have someone to take my place."

"I wouldn't have you jeopardize your career just for the sake of Joy's Dance Studio. Joy would never have heard of it either. We'll work something out." Letty was surprised to find out Kathleen already had a contingency plan in place.

Chloe hadn't been surprised when Kathleen called as soon as she finished talking to Letty.

"Chloe, how would you like to work full-time at the dance studio? I need someone to take Letty's place."

"But what about the trip to Ireland?"

"We can work around it. I'll close for that week if I have to. Can you teach jazz and modern dance?"

"I've had plenty of lessons, just never taught it."

"And what about advanced ballet classes?"

"Same thing."

"Don't worry. I'll work something out. Maybe Letty can help you with it before she leaves."

Letty gave Chloe a crash course in teaching dance before heading out to New York that September. Chloe talked it over with her grandfather and they decided to postpone their trip until the spring.

"Besides, if Ashley gets into the International Competition, we can combine that with a trip to Northern Ireland."

It seemed Chloe now had a job and a reason to stay a while longer.

Chapter 37

Ashley did well in both of the summer competitions. Her whole family had come to those but only Ava was going with her to the Oireachtas, the National Champion Competition, in the Chicago area that November.

"I'm sorry, Ashley. I have to work. Besides it's too long and far to take Jacob and Grace. Someone has to take care of them," Dale had explained.

"Grandma and Grandpa can watch them."

"You think that just because we are spending the weekend together, we'll come back friends."

"Maybe, but I still have to work."

"Why can't I ride with Chloe and Aunt Kathleen?"

"Because Uncle Howard and the baby are going with them. There won't be enough room in their car. You'll have fun with Ava."

"It will be a girls' weekend," Ava added. "Besides, who will do your hair? Your dad can't do that." Contestants wore long curly locks. Many of the girls wore wigs which had to be firmly attached lest they come loose during the competition. Ashley opted to have her own long blonde hair curled.

"Chloe can do it."

"Ashley, you are going with Ava and that's final. Either you go with Ava or you don't go at all," Dale asserted.

"Fine, can I go now?"

"Go," Dale said. Ashley stomped off upstairs.

"That didn't go well," Ava said after she was gone. "You know, Ashley clearly doesn't want to go with me. Maybe we can work out something else. This is her big weekend. Maybe Kathleen can take her."

"No, Chloe will need help with the baby. Besides we already discussed this. Ashley has to learn to accept you as part of the family."

"I know, but it's an awful long drive to spend with an angry pre-teen."

"You'll manage," he kissed her hand. "When are you going to start wearing that ring I gave you?"

Ava sighed, "Maybe once I know Ashley will be okay with it."

"This is as good a time as any."

"We'll see how the weekend goes," Ava told him.

It was a long drive to Chicago. Ava tried to make small talk at first. Ashley maintained a stony silence.

"I know what you and Dad are up to," Ashley finally said.

"What do you mean?"

"I think your dad thinks so."

"Not gonna happen."

"Okay. We don't have to be friends. Do you think we could get along? We might even be able to have some fun."

"Sure, whatever you say." Ashley retreated back into silence.

"Feel free to set the radio to the station you want," Ava told her. Ashley popped on her headphone and listened to her music.

The competition ran from Friday to Sunday. Dancers were arriving from all over the Midwest for their chance to go to the World Competition in Dublin that spring. Patrick had a group coming with him in the school van. Michelle and Jessica, another dancer from Ashley's class, were competing in the teen division. They rode with Michelle's dad, Pastor Joe. They were staying at the same hotel with Ashley, as well as Chloe and those in her car. When they met for dinner Friday night after getting settled into their rooms, Ashley was all too happy to get away from Ava and join Michelle and Jessica.

"Don't worry. You might as well get used to it," Joe told Ava when he saw her standing alone in the hotel lobby. "The last thing any teenager wants is to be with their parents."

"I'm not exactly a parent."

"You are the parent in loco," Joe joked. Ava didn't smile.

"At least other parents have had all that time when the kids were little and liked having them around to build a bond. I don't have any of that with Ashley."

"These things take time," Joe reassured her. They joined the rest of their group and went out for Chicago style pizza before the opening of the oireachtas. Ashly reluctantly went back to her room with Ava afterwards.

"Why can't I stay with Michelle and Jessica?" she whined.

"There isn't enough room."

"I can sleep on the floor."

"You need to get a good night's sleep before the competition tomorrow. After that we'll talk about it."

They were up early for breakfast then signed in and found out when and where they were dancing. Ashley joined the other girls from Patrick's school that were dancing in her age group. Patrick had set up a "camp" of sorts for his dancers, as did the other schools represented. It was a place for the dancers to hang out in between dances, warm-up, practice or just talk.

Each dancer in Ashley's group was scheduled to dance twice, once in soft shoes and once in hard shoes. The top dancers would be called back on Sunday for the final competition. Ashley was confident she'd make it into the final. She had ended in first or second place in each of the competitions she had entered so far, but as she watched the girls from so many other dance schools perform, she began to have doubts. Some wore elaborate costumes with wigs that made their hair look three times the size of her hair. The older girls were loaded with make-up. Ashley's age group wasn't allowed to wear make-up.

"They look ridiculous," Ashley whispered to Chloe as they watched the parade of costumes.

"It does seem a bit much, all the costumes, big hair and make-up. I don't remember it being quite so bad when I danced, but that was almost twelve years ago."

"Do you miss it?" Ava asked.

"I have some good memories from dancing in competitions, but do I miss it? Nah. It was fun, but that was long ago."

Kathleen came to get Ashley. "You're going to be up soon. You have to get in place." Ashley smoothed down her dress and shook her curls.

"Do I look okay?"

"You look great," Ava told her. Ashley ignored the comment and followed Kathleen. Ava, Howard, Chloe and the baby proceeded to the auditorium to watch. Each dancer was given a number which was pinned on their costume so the judges could easily identify them. No names were listed when showing points earned, just the numbers. Three dancers came out at a time, danced for 48 bars of music, which wasn't much time. They then waited until they were dismissed by the judges. It was pretty intense. A lot of practice went into those 48 bars.

They had to be perfect. No room for a single slip up or misstep. If you got off to a bad start, or if the music wasn't at the tempo you expected, they was no making up for it.

Ashley's dance came off without a flaw, as far as Ava could tell. But then so many of the dancers were so good.

"How can they judge with so little time?" she asked Chloe.

"There are specific things each judge looks for. How straight the dancer stands, her overall demeanor. Whether they do all of the required steps. How high are the kicks. Ashley's training in ballet was good practice for Irish step dancing. More and more they are requiring going on your toes and moves associated with ballet. The competition gets harder each year. Ashley did fine."

Ashley appeared pleased with her performance as well. "Did you see that girl to the right of me?"

"What were you doing looking to your right? You are supposed to focus ahead of you the whole time," Chloe reprimanded her.

"I saw it out of the corner of my eye. She messed up."

"You were great," Howard told her as she sat down and waited through the next few dancers before getting her score. She was easily in the top ten.

The afternoon went pretty much the same. They watched Michelle and Jessica dance after Ashley's dances.

"How are they doing?" Chloe asked Joe when they joined him.

"I think they are great, but you better ask them."

"I don't think I'll get in the second round," Michelle said, "but that's okay. It was fun to compete. I'm just not as good as those others girls. Some of them have been dancing since they were five or six."

Michelle sat by her father while Jessica danced. She glanced over at Kathleen who was sitting one row up and further down the row from them, then glanced back at her dad.

"Dad," she got his attention. "You and Kathleen . . ."

"Not going to happen. Don't want to talk about it." Joe cut her off before she could say anything, trying to focus on the dancers.

"You didn't let me finish."

"I know what you are going to say and I don't want to talk about it. Subject closed."

"But, Dad, what I was going to say, was that Stephanie wants me to try to get you two back together. She told me it was my responsibility to do that for her since she was gone away to college."

"That's a ridiculous idea."

"That's what I told her. I told her that it was none of our business who you dated. Besides, Kathleen isn't right for you anyway."

"Oh, why do you say that?" Joe looked over at his daughter.

"You said it yourself, you are too different." This time Michelle was the one looking at the dancers.

"Oh, yeah, that's right." Joe returned his gaze to the stage. "You really think so?"

"Sure. I mean, she doesn't even go to church. She's a little on the wild side, isn't she, Dad?"

"Yeah," he agreed. It was nothing different from what he had said himself at times, but hearing it come from his daughter, it suddenly sounded like a challenge. He shifted uncomfortably in his seat and gazed over at Kathleen then quickly looked away lest she catch him staring at her. The corners of Michelle's lips turned up in a slight smile as she saw her dad looking at Kathleen.

Neither Michelle nor Jessica made it into the final round.

"Don't be discouraged," Patrick told them. "You can come back next year. Another year of practice will make a world of difference." Michelle had already decided there wouldn't be a next year. Once was enough. This year was fun, but there were far too many other activities for a high school student that Irish dancing interfered with.

They met again that night to celebrate Ashley's success.

"You're going to stay and watch me, aren't you?" Ashley asked Michelle and Jessica.

"We didn't come all this way to go home early," Joe told her, responding for the girls.

"What do you think, Howard?" Kathleen asked. "Is this anything like what you saw in Ireland in the '40s?"

"Not at all. There were no costumes and dancers sometimes danced in their bare feet. At least that's how I remember Chloe's grandmother."

"Tell Michelle and Jessica about it, Uncle Howard." Ashley loved Howard's stories.

"Not much to tell. I saw her dancing and fell in love."

"There's more than that to the story," Chloe said. "They were separated for years, almost married other people before they finally ended up together."

"What was important was that we ended up together."

"How did you end up together after all of that?" Kathleen asked.

"Don't know. I guess it was what the good Lord intended. We slipped into a relationship at first. It was so right and easy. Sure we had our problems. It was especially hard being separated by hundreds of miles of water. Chloe's grandmother didn't want to leave Ireland and I couldn't leave America. We fought about it, broke up, then something happened to change your grandmother's mind. I never knew exactly what it was. She never told me, but somehow we got back together and were together ever since, over sixty years of marriage."

"Did you fight ever?" Ashley asked.

"Did we! That's what kept the marriage interesting," Howard laughed. "That Irish temper of Chloe's grandmother. There were days when I could do no right, but other days when we would laugh and dance . . . They were good times. I always thought I was a little too stodgy for your grandma, but she loved me anyway. She had to create a row now and then, had to stir things up. Sometimes things need stirring up."

"So it wasn't all peace and tranquility?" Kathleen asked.

"What relationship is? They've all got their bumps to work out."

"I thought you and Helen never fought, at least that was the impression you gave me with your stories," Kathleen said.

"Oh, they fought all right." Chloe responded to Kathleen's comment. "I can remember some major battles when I was a little girl visiting. Grandpa never wanted to fight, but Grandma wouldn't let him get away with avoiding it."

"I was the peacemaker. She wouldn't let me get away with that. She kept me in line. I miss that." Howard began to get up. "And now, I think it's time I get some sleep,"

"Okay, Grandpa," Chloe got up as well. Howard was looking tired after the long drive yesterday and long day today. "Maybe you should sleep in tomorrow. Get your rest before the drive home," she told him as he prepared for bed.

"And miss Ashley's dance? Nonsense, I'm fine."

As the rest of the group finished their meal, Ashley asked again about staying with Michelle and Jessica.

"You are still competing tomorrow. You need a good night's sleep," Ava told her.

"Can I at least ride home with them?" Chloe looked over at Joe for help before saying, "I'll think about it and let you know."

She called Dale that night and let him know how Ashley did.

"That's great, and how are you doing?"

"Okay, I guess. Ashley wants to ride home with Michelle and Jessica and their dad."

"No, she came with you, she'll go home with you. I don't want you driving home alone."

"Dale, it's not working. I'll be fine by myself."

"That's not the point. Ashley has got to learn."

"And I'm the one here dealing with the situation." This statement was met with silence on the phone. Finally Dale responded.

"Okay, do what you think best."

"You know I always do."

Howard insisted on attending the morning competition even though he wasn't feeling well. "I'll have plenty of time to sleep when I'm dead," he told Chloe.

"Grandpa, don't talk like that, not even joking. You're going to be around for a lot more years. You have to watch Mary grow up."

"I don't think that I'll be around that long, but I would like a few more years," he responded.

He sat with the group waiting for Ashley to come on stage to dance her two dances. As he watched, it seemed he was back in Ireland, watching another young girl dance, watching Mary Helen just as she had been when they first met, barefoot and dancing in the grass. It seemed the room around him dissolved into air and all he saw was her.

Suddenly she stopped and reached out her hand for his. "It's waiting I've been. What took you so long?"

He stumbled, unable to get up at first. Then he realized his body wasn't the same body he had woken up with that morning. His body was young again, as young as when he had first met Mary Helen.

"Come you on," Mary Helen called to him. "What are you waiting for?" With that, Howard stood up, took her hand and they walked away together.

Chapter 38

Everyone was clapping at the end of the dance. Chloe looked over at Howard to see how he was doing and saw his body slumped as if asleep.

"Grandpa?" Chloe gently shook him to wake him up. "Grandpa," she said again as he didn't move.

"Something's wrong," she told Kathleen. "He won't wake up. We've got to get the paramedics."

Joe got up from his seat and called for an ambulance. The medical staff that were on call at the conference center cleared out the people next to Howard as they checked for a pulse.

"Uncle Howard," Ashley said as she returned from the stage to join the group. Ava stopped her as they prepared to take Howard out on a stretcher.

"It's okay, Ashley," Chloe assured her. "We are taking Grandpa to the hospital. He'll be okay. You stay here with Ava." Michelle took Mary from Chloe so she could go with the ambulance.

Joe offered to drive Kathleen to the hospital. "Michelle and Jessica can stay with Ava and Ashley," he told her.

By the time they reached the hospital, it was apparent that it was too late. The paramedics had administered CPR and tried to jolt Howard's heart back, but were unsuccessful. The emergency room physician pronounced him dead on arrival.

"What do I do now?" Chloe asked as Joe hugged her. "It's my fault. I never should have let him come on this trip. I knew it might be too much for him."

"Chloe, there's no way you could have stopped him. You know how determined he was to see Ashley dance," Kathleen said.

"Besides, it may have happened at home and you wouldn't have been there. You just don't know about these things. You can't blame yourself," Joe added.

"I have to call my parents," Chloe said as she quieted down. "They need to know."

Chloe's dad arranged for a flight that night. Her mother was going to meet them at Cascade Falls as soon as she could get away.

"You don't have to stay. My dad will be here tonight," Chloe told Kathleen and Joe. "Pastor Joe, do you think you could give Kathleen a ride home?"

"Of course, I can."

Ashley hadn't wanted to stay at the competition. She wanted to go to the hospital with Kathleen, but Chloe had insisted.

"My grandfather would never forgive me if I let this keep you from getting your award. You stay here. I'll let you know how he is as soon as I know."

Ashley waited with Ava, Michelle and Jessica for her score. When all the scores were calculated she was in second place.

"Ashley, that's wonderful," Michelle said as she hugged her. Ashley didn't respond at first.

"Congratulations, Ashley." Patrick joined them. "You have to attend the awards ceremony," he told her. "And now you are qualified for the World Competition." Three other dancers from his school had also qualified.

Ashley posed with her trophy, standing next to the first-place winner. "See you in Dublin," she said to Ashley when they were done getting their pictures taken. Ashley didn't respond. She walked over to Ava, carrying her trophy.

"How's Uncle Howard?" she asked. Michelle and Jessica looked to Ava, waiting for her to tell Ashley.

"I'm sorry, Ashley. He didn't make it."

Ashley let go of the trophy and let Ava wrap her arms around her while she cried. Ava waited quietly, allowing Ashley's tears to flow freely as she wiped away tears of her own.

"I want to go home. Can we go now?" Ashley said through her tears.

Ava looked at Michelle and Jessica.

"Go ahead," Michelle shifted Mary on her hip. "My dad's on his way to pick us up then we'll be leaving too. You don't have to wait for us."

Ava gathered Ashley's trophy and dance costume as she changed in the bathroom. She had already packed the car after checking out of the hotel that morning. She had figured they could always move bags later if Ashley were to ride home with Joe. All they needed to do was get on the road.

Chapter 39

"Can I have some time alone with my grandfather?" Chloe asked the staff at the emergency room.

"Yes, you can," an orderly took her to the room where Howard's body lay. He looked peaceful lying there. Chloe touched his skin and spoke his name to assure herself he was no longer alive. The skin was clammy to the touch.

"Grandpa, how could you leave me now, just when I was getting my life back together? What will I do now?" she silently asked him. He did not respond.

"Or are you just trying to knock me off balance, like you said Grandma did to you? Is this just a misstep in my life to be gotten over? Or a major upheaval? I know what my mom will want me to do."

"It depends on how you choose to deal with this. What do you want to do?" It seemed she could hear him responding as he always did.

"I don't know."

"You can't keep slipping through life, letting circumstances determine your life. You need to take charge of your own life," he said as he had told her so many times in the past.

"How can I do that when I don't know what I want? How can I stay in Cascades Falls without you?"

Her grandfather remained silent on the matter. She remembered talking to him about Mary shortly after she had first arrived.

"It was a mistake. I'm not ready for a baby. I can hardly manage my own life. How can I manage someone else's life?"

"Is it a mistake? Or maybe one of those fortuitous slip-ups where God gets us to where we are meant to be? Perhaps it was no mistake at all but part of God's plan for your life."

When her grandfather had said that, Chloe hadn't believed it. How could this be God's plan? But now, when she thought about holding Mary in her arms, she knew it couldn't be a mistake. This little baby was not a mistake. Or if she was a mistake, she was a blessed mistake. How could that not be God's plan for her?

But if that was God's plan, how does her grandfather's death fit into the plan? Surely it wasn't God's plan to take him away from her when she needed him most.

"You can do it," Howard's voice echoed in her head. "You don't need me anymore. You can make it on your own, make your own decisions."

"With a baby?"

"Yes, with a baby. I'm needed elsewhere."

"We have to stop doing this," Kathleen told Joe as they sat in the waiting room.

"Doing what?"

"All these crises. It seems we are always being thrown together by crisis."

"Maybe God is trying to tell us something." Joe cocked his head at her and raised an eyebrow.

"I don't know about that."

"Then what do you think this is about?"

"I don't know but I'll tell you as soon as I have it figured out."

"You do that. Maybe you're the right person to upset my nice and tidy life."

"Nice and tidy? Since when is life with a teenager nice and tidy? What are you talking about?"

"What Howard said last night about how Helen kept his life interesting, kept upsetting the apple cart."

"He didn't say anything about an apple cart."

"It was implied. You are definitely good at challenging some of my preconceptions."

"And that's good?"

"Very good," Joe smiled.

"Nice to know I'm good for something. So you're saying we could be good for each other? How are you good for me?"

"I'm the peacemaker, providing stability to your life."

"Hmmm," Kathleen wasn't sure what she thought about that.

"Do you want to give it another try?" He waited as Kathleen pondered the question.

"Maybe," she finally responded.

"Just maybe?"

"Just maybe."

"I guess that's better than a no," Joe shook his head in acceptance.

Chloe dried her eyes, said goodbye and returned to the waiting room where Kathleen and Joe were waiting to take her back to the Oireachtas to pick up Mary.

Chapter 40

Ashley was silent for the first hour of the drive.

"I'm really sorry, Ashley," Ava finally broke the silence, repeating what she had said earlier.

"It's my fault."

"How is it your fault?"

"I wanted Uncle Howard to come. If he had stayed home, he would have been okay."

"We don't know that, Ashley. He may have died anyway."

"Why do the people I love leave me?"

"Uncle Howard was old, over ninety. He couldn't live forever."

"My mom wasn't old."

Ava searched for words. "I guess I'm not the best person to talk to about this. I've had losses, mostly from my own mistakes, but I've never had someone I love die. My parents and grandparents are still alive."

"You're okay," Ashley told her without a glance in her direction.

"I'm glad to hear you think so."

"It's just better not to get too close."

"I don't know if this helps or not, but I promise I won't leave you."

"No, it doesn't help. And you can't promise that. You and dad will break-up and then you'll be gone." Ashley continued to stare straight ahead.

"Can I tell you a secret?"

"What?" Ashley glanced over in Ava's direction.

"Your dad asked me to marry him."

"Oh, so are you?" She looked back at the road ahead of them.

"I don't know. I told him I had to okay it with you first." Ava glanced at Ashley.

"Why with me?" Ashley turned to look at her.

"Because I'm not just marrying your dad. I'm marrying into a family." Ava focused back on the road.

"Did he give you a ring?"

"Yes."

"Not my mother's ring?"

"No, that's yours. Your dad is keeping it for you someday."

"Can I see it, the ring?"

"Sure, if I can get it out of my pocket." Ava had been keeping it in her pocket to squeeze every now and then as a reminder of Dale's love. She had squeezed it a lot that weekend. She fumbled in her pocket while keeping her eyes on the road ahead of her. She pulled the ring out along with a chap stick she kept in her pocket. The ring slipped, bounced off the divider between the seats and rolled on the floor.

"I guess you'll have to get it to see it," she told Ashley. Ashley unbuckled and felt around on the floor until she found it.

"Pretty," she said, rolling it around in her hand and trying it on, before snapping the seatbelt back on. "Why aren't you wearing it?"

"I told your dad I wouldn't wear it until you said it was okay."

"Oh," Ashley pondered for a while. "Okay."

"What?"

"I said okay. You can put the ring on."

"Does that mean you are okay with me being part of your family?"

"I guess if not you, it would be somebody else. At least I'm used to you."

Tears formed in Ava's eyes. She blinked them back before answering. "All right then."

"Here. You better put this on before you lose it." Ashley gave her back the ring, helping Ava slip it on her finger.

"Now I really can't leave you," Ava smiled over at Ashley. Ashley squirmed then reached for the radio to find a station she liked.

Ava had called Dale before they left Chicago and let him know what had happened to Howard. Lucky was waiting at the door when they arrived. He licked Ashley and stayed by her side. Ashley excused herself and went upstairs, followed by Lucky.

"It's as if he knows," Dale commented. "How was the ride home?"

"Okay, better than okay," Ava raised her hand to show the ring.

"What happened?"

"Ashley said it was okay for me to wear it."

"Does this mean the wedding's on?"

“I guess it does.”

He started to kiss her then paused. “You know, Ashley will still be difficult. She’s not even a teenager yet.”

“I know, but I will have you to help me through those years.”

“And for many more years,” he said as they kissed.

Chapter 41

Chloe's dad called his sister. She was flying to Chicago as well, but not till much later. Jimmy had already made some arrangements by phone before even getting on the plane.

Chloe met him at the airport. They drove together to the hospital.

"I'd like to see him before they take him to the funeral home," he told Chloe. He had called a couple of funeral homes and made arrangements with one. They were just waiting for his okay to come get the body.

"Did Grandpa ever tell you what he wanted for his funeral?"

"No. We talked about so many things, but never that."

"Well, Grandma was cremated. I suspect that's what he would want as well. We'll talk it over with your Aunt Meghan when she gets here. It would be easier to have the cremation done here then have the ashes shipped to Cascades Falls, or wherever."

Aunt Meghan came in like a cyclone and started to take charge.

"We already have a funeral home," Jim informed her as they shared a late-night snack after her flight. "We need to meet with them tomorrow to work out details."

"We cremated Mom so I'm thinking we do the same for Dad."

"That's what we were thinking."

"What about the service?"

"We didn't know about that. Dad was Presbyterian. We could contact the Presbyterian church," Jim suggested.

"Yes, but he wasn't exactly a practicing Presbyterian. I don't remember him ever going to church when we were kids except for the times he came with us on holidays or special occasions."

"Pastor Joe knows him," Chloe suggested.

"Is he Presbyterian?"

"No, I think he's Lutheran. I never asked."

"No, that won't do. Am I the only practicing Catholic in this family?" Meghan asked. Jim and Chloe exchanged glances. "I thought so. I think we should have the service in the Catholic Church. It's what Mom would have wanted." Jim didn't argue with that.

"But will we even be able to have the service in a Catholic Church since he wasn't Catholic?" Jim asked.

"I'll take care of that. And while we are on the subject, have you baptized that baby yet?" Mary was sleeping quietly in her car seat while the adults talked. As if on cue, she wriggled and smiled.

"No," Chloe said, "I've thought about it, just haven't done anything yet."

"We can have the baptism around the same time as the Memorial Service. You were going to baptize her Catholic, weren't you?"

"I haven't decided yet. Pastor Joe is a friend. I thought maybe ..."

"No maybe. She'll be Catholic. Mom wouldn't have it any other way." Chloe wanted to object but she knew her Aunt Meghan was right. It was what her grandmother would have wanted.

"I'll talk to the priest about it. I don't suppose you know who that is?" Again Chloe and Jim looked at each other. "I didn't think so. I'll take care of it." Meghan was writing notes to herself while her brother and niece looked on.

"We don't have to have the service right away. Still it would be nice to have it before Christmas. I'll see when my kids will be free to come to Michigan." She made another notation. "Now about the house, we'll have to clean it out, figure out what to do with all of the furniture, maybe have an estate sale."

"Wait a minute, Meghan," Jim interrupted her.

"What's wrong? You don't want the house do you? I know I don't." At this Chloe started to cry.

"Dad isn't even in the grave and you're dividing the spoils."

"I have limited time to be here. I'm just trying to get as much done as possible while I'm here."

"This can wait until tomorrow, or at least till we get home."

"That house isn't my home. It never was. It was just the house Dad moved Mom into."

"But it has been Chloe's home for the past year." Jim put his arm around Chloe. "She just lost her grandfather, do we have to take her home away just yet?"

"Fine," Meghan closed her notebook. "But we will need to take care of it eventually."

They sat in silence for a few minutes.

"So, Chloe," Meghan began. "I hear you've been teaching dance classes. How is that going?"

Chloe started to cry again.

"I think it's time to call it a night." Jim reached for the bill. "It's been a long day for all of us."

They met with the funeral director the next morning, made arrangements for the cremation, then drove to Cascades Falls together where they met Chloe's mom. Nora bristled when she saw Meghan, the tornado meeting the cyclone.

"Meghan," she said, extending her hand.

"Nora," Meghan took her hand. "Good of you to drive all this way."

"He was my father-in-law," Nora said as they walked into the house and settled in.

"I guess there's nothing more we can do tonight," Meghan said after dinner. "I suppose there's a will somewhere. We need to check that. I'll contact the Catholic Church tomorrow."

"I've got a copy of the will. I brought it with me. Dad made me executor," Jim said.

"He did?"

"I was the closest family member." Jim did not want to play out this game with his sister. As kids he had always been mamma's boy, and she had been daddy's girl. But that had changed as adults, at least where he was concerned. "At least it's the last will I know about. I'll check with his lawyer to make sure he hadn't updated it."

Meghan got up from the table and walked around the living room, examining pictures, memorabilia.

"Staking your claim?" Jim said.

"I'm not that bad, am I?" Meghan didn't wait for an answer. She started to cry, "I can't believe he's gone." She looked away from her brother as she fought the tears, randomly picking up objects then putting them back down.

"I can't believe it either," her brother replied. Meghan straightened her shoulders, wiped her tears, shook her head and frowned as if looking for a fight.

"Mom hated this house."

"I don't remember it like that. Why do you say that?"

"She told me so. She couldn't find anything, couldn't remember where anything was."

"That was because of the Alzheimer's."

"Maybe, but it wouldn't have been so bad if she had stayed in her own home."

"Why do you insist on bringing this up?"

"Because it's true."

"And if they had stayed in that old three-story farmhouse, eventually one of them would have fallen down the stairs at some time."

"Possibly. I guess we'll never know." Meghan continued to sniffle as she turned away from Jimmy again to avoid his eyes.

"Do you have any idea how much like Mom you are?"

"I'm not like Mom. You are more like Mom than me."

"No, you just can't leave well enough alone, always have to be stirring up trouble."

"Am I really like that?" Meghan glanced at the three of them.

"Yes," all three answered.

"I just try to get things done. No sense in hiding behind sentimentality. I just speak the truth." Meghan wiped her eyes, hiding from the truth they had spoken.

"No matter who it may hurt," Jim said. Meghan smiled at this despite her tears.

"Maybe I am more like Mom than I thought. I did love her. And I love Dad. I wish I didn't live so far away. And now they are both gone. All I have left is you, baby brother, and you live far away too." Meghan began to cry again.

"But that doesn't mean we can't visit."

"But will we?"

"We will if it's important enough to both of us."

"I will if you will," Meghan promised and hugged Jimmy.

Meghan and Jimmy spent the rest of the evening sharing stories about growing up with their mom and dad while Chloe and Nora listened.

"You never wanted to visit Ireland?" Jim asked as the night got late.

"No, that was your thing. You always liked all things Irish. Got it from Mom."

"Maybe that was just your way of rebelling."

"Maybe back then, but not anymore. I've got a full life, kids and grandkids. I don't feel the need to go traipsing across the world. What about you? Why haven't you gone?"

"Never seemed to have the time. We were going to go, me and Chloe with Dad. It didn't work out." Jim looked over at Chloe. "Maybe this spring we'll go. We'll take Mom and Dad's ashes. One last visit for both of them. Do you want to come with us?" he asked Meghan.

"I'll think about it, but probably not." Chloe retreated to her bedroom with Mary. Jim and Nora set up camp in the basement, leaving Meghan her dad's room. It just didn't feel right, sleeping in his bed now that he was gone. She ended up on the couch in the living room.

Chapter 42

Chloe had had her experience dancing on Broadway and years of classes, but that hadn't prepared her for teaching others. It had been a stiff learning curve for her. Her time assisting in classes last year proved helpful, especially the guidance she had received from Letty. Other than that, she was learning as she went. There were also administrative details, hiring and supervising other instructors, making sure they were paid, collecting monthly fees. Kathleen helped with some of this, but others were largely her own responsibility.

Still she had been excited when the first day of class arrived. She had been surprised when the police officer she had met over the summer showed up with a three-year-old to enroll in one of the beginner classes.

"I didn't realize you were married. You don't have a ring on your finger."

"That's because I'm not. This is my sister's daughter. She's not able to take care of her right now so I'm helping out. What about you?"

"What about me?"

"You married?"

"No, I'm not." Officer Nash nodded at Mary, sleeping in her car seat. "Mary is mine. It's a long story."

"I'd love to hear it some time, maybe over dinner."

"Sure," Chloe said. "You know where you can reach me." Chloe had been disappointed when he hadn't called but too busy with the dance studio to spend too much time on it.

"What am I going to do for the Christmas program?" Chloe had asked Letty. Letty called on a regular basis to hear what was happening at the dance studio and to update Chloe on her progress with Ailey II. "And the recital? I've never put together a recital before. I've only choreographed dances for myself, never a whole school."

"Relax. I'll help. I'm getting lots of great ideas here, when I have time to think, in between classes and rehearsals," Letty told her. "Sit down with the other instructors and brainstorm ideas for an overall theme. Then each instructor choreographs dances for their own classes. You only have to take care of the classes you are teaching."

“That’s a relief.”

“I’ll help out when I come home for the holidays,” Letty assured her.

With all of her new responsibilities, taking care of her baby, and now her grandfather’s death, Chloe had little free time for wondering why Officer Nash didn’t call, much less time for dating. Now and then she caught a glimpse of him picking up his niece. Most of the time other family members took care of this.

She spent the first few weeks after her grandfather’s death in a state of numbness. She just couldn’t believe he was gone. By the time of the Memorial Service, the numbness had worn off, leaving a raw ache in its place. The ache was relieved some by the support she received from her friends at the Dance Studio. She was surprised by the number of people who attended the service, including Officer Nash.

“I’m sorry for your loss,” he said as he shook her hand.

“Did you know my grandfather?”

“Some. Not a lot but enough to know I wanted to pay my respects.”

“He was a good man,” Chloe said.

“Yes, that much I know. I’m also sorry I haven’t called you yet. It was my intention to call. My life got very busy.”

“I know about that.”

“I would like to make it up to you, maybe take you out next weekend?” Chloe looked over at her parents and realized they were waiting for her to join them.

“Yes, I would like that. Call me,” she shook his hand again.

“Who was that?” her mother asked.

“Just a friend of Grandpa’s”

“Seems your grandpa had a lot of friends, more than we realized,” her dad said. They had not expected a large crowd for the Mass. At ninety, so many of Howard’s friends his own age were gone. There hadn’t been a large crowd at Helen’s service, just immediate family. They hadn’t counted on all the new friends Howard had made through his involvement with the dance studio.

Dale and Ava came with his three children. “Our dog, Lucky, was your dad’s dog. He let us have him when my children’s mother was dying from cancer. He truly was a part of our family. My kids all called him Uncle Howard. Ashley, here, was especially close to him." Dale shook Jim's hand.

"So this is the young dancer I've heard so much about." Jim reached for Ashley's hand. "The one helping with my grandchild." Ashley quietly shook his hand.

"He was definitely a part of the family," Esther shook Jim's hand as well. "I'm Dale's mother, Ashley's Grandmother. We invited your dad to all of our family events, including Thanksgiving, birthdays and our wedding. It won't be the same without him." With each expression of affection for his father from people he didn't know, Jim found tears rising to the surface, tears of sadness and admiration for a side of his dad he had not known. He glanced over at his sister who was fighting her own tears.

"He's been such a great help at the dance studio, helping out with repairs," Kathleen added. "We are going to miss him." Kathleen had come with Pastor Joe. They had decided this was something they could do together.

"It involves going to church, not just church, but a Catholic Church," Joe had questioned her. With the promise of a baptism and Chloe's promise to start attending church and bring Mary up Catholic, the priest had been talked into having the service in the church.

"It's what my grandmother would have wanted," Chloe had told Fr. Anthony. Fr. Anthony had barely known Helen, having arrived at St. Paul's after she had been placed in the Alzheimer's unit. But he had done her Memorial Mass and remembered Howard so had agreed to the arrangements.

"Is it that different?" Kathleen asked. "Howard's one of the few people I will go to church for."

"Not for me?"

"Maybe if you were dead."

"Hmmmm, even for the saving of your soul, I don't know if it would be worth it."

"You know I only go to weddings and funerals."

"Well, a Catholic Mass will be different from the services you've attended before. I'll help you out." Joe prodded her when to stand up, when to sit down, when to kneel. When it came time for communion, he grabbed her before she went up. "Only Catholics can receive communion at a Catholic Mass. You can receive a blessing, if you want, but you have to cross your hands in front of your chest to let the priest know you want a blessing. Didn't you listen to what the priest had said?"

Kathleen remembered the priest going on about something but hadn't listened. She looked around at the rest of her family members and those attending from the dance studio and saw they were sitting down so she stayed in her seat.

"Now that would have been something if you had gone up for communion. Maybe I should have let you. Maybe the grace in the sacrament would have done you some good."

"I was just trying to follow along with everybody else. All of that standing and sitting and kneeling. It was confusing."

Members of the staff at the dance studio and Chloe's students attended as well, standing awkwardly together, unsure how to behave at a Memorial Service. One by one they came over and hugged Chloe before leaving.

"I'm so glad you aren't leaving the school," they told her. There had been some concern that after her grandfather's death, Chloe would leave Cascade Falls. Kathleen, always preparing contingency plans, had been racking her brain for someone to fill in. She had been relieved when Chloe told her she was staying.

"Grandpa left me the house. It was his wish that I stay here, so I'm staying for the time being," Chloe had told Kathleen.

"Well, you have a job as long as you want," Kathleen assured her.

"That's good to know." The news that Howard had left his house to her had not been well received by her mother or her aunt.

"Did you know about this?" Meghan had asked Chloe after meeting with the lawyer and reading Howard's latest will.

"No, Grandpa never said anything about this. I knew he wanted me to stay here with Mary, but that was with him." Howard had updated his will a month before his death, leaving the house and all of its furnishings to Chloe, along with a sum of money, enough for her to live off of for five years or more if she was careful.

"Clearly Grandpa wanted you to live here, but that doesn't mean you have to. You can sell the house and move back in with us until you decide what to do," her mother informed her.

"I know, Mom. I'll think about it."

She had thought about it, and the more she thought about it, the more she realized she didn't want to leave Cascades Falls, not now, maybe not ever. She had friends here, friends that were like family. And it was a good place to raise a baby. The prospect of staying alone in the house had been daunting at first. She kept waiting for her grandfather to show up, surprise her, tell her it had all been a bad dream. When that didn't happen, she grew accustomed to the quiet.

Sorting through some of her grandfather's papers, she found an Irish saying, written in her grandmother's hand.

"Your feet will bring you to where your heart is." She pulled it out of the papers, looked at it again, then placed it in the book of Gaelic prayers from her grandmother.

Funny, she had always thought her heart would guide her feet to where she was meant to be. But no, it had been her feet, her dancing feet that had brought her to this point in her life, just as her grandmother's dancing feet had caught the eye of a young soldier and led across the ocean to America. Her feet had led Chloe home and here she would stay.

Epilogue

The family signed in at the hotel in downtown Belfast.

"Will you be staying long?" the clerk asked.

"Just a few days, then we are going to drive along the coast, explore Northern Ireland before heading for home."

"I hope you enjoy your stay here," he said as he finished checking them in. Chloe shifted Mary on her hip. Mary wasn't walking yet but at not quite a year, she had gotten to be quite heavy to carry. Mary wasn't content to remain in her carrier or her mom's lap and wanted down to crawl. Chloe's mom had been talked into coming on the trip to help with the baby. Chloe was grateful for the help.

"My mother was from Belfast. We are going to visit family, places where she lived and worked. Her father, my grandfather, used to work in this hotel as a cook," Jim explained.

"Did he? What was his name?"

"Thomas Maguire."

"I'm afraid that was before my time. Do you need any help locating your family or finding places?"

"I think we are all set. I've got addresses and phone numbers for my Aunt Brigid and some of my cousins. If we need help, I'll be sure to ask."

Ashley had decided not to go to the Worlds. Chloe had been disappointed but nowhere near as much as Patrick.

"She has the natural ability. She could take it all. If not this year, then in a year or two. She's throwing away a God-given gift."

"You'll have to tell her that. I won't," Chloe had told him. Patrick had tried to convince her to change her mind but Ashley wouldn't budge.

"I like Irish step dance, but I think I'll go back to ballet. It reminds me of my mother," she had told Chloe.

"You can do both, you know."

"I know, but I kind of want to try some other things. Some of my friends at school are talking about forming a band. I talked to my dad about guitar lessons. He said he would think about it, but I would have to give something up."

"So, it's the Irish dancing you're giving up."

"I like the dancing, but I don't care for the costumes and the hair. I can still dance for fun, can't I?"

"Of course you can." Ashley had wanted to come along with them on this trip but her dad had decided she was too young just yet.

"You can't be missing school and the wedding is coming up. You're going to be a junior bridesmaid. You can't do everything," her dad had told her.

"We'll come another time. Maybe you can come with us then," Chloe had told her.

Armed with all the stories Howard had told her, they found the shirt factory where her grandma had worked and the house on Whiterock where she had grown up. It had been sold out of the family when her great grandparents had died. They knocked on the door to see if anyone was home.

"If you please, my mother used to live here. We were wondering if we could see inside, if it's not too much of an imposition." A woman holding a baby with another child at her feet, answered the door. She was about to say no when she saw Mary in Chloe's arms.

"You have a wee one, too. How old is she?"

"Not quite a year."

"Mine is just six months."

"Would you mind if we looked around? We don't have to go upstairs, but if I could see the kitchen?" Chloe remembered her grandmother's stories about the kitchen.

The woman paused then agreed. "Seeing as you're a mother yourself, you'll understand the mess."

"That I do."

She showed them to the kitchen. "You know this place was burned down during the troubles."

"No, I didn't," Jim said.

"They were able to rebuild it. It wasn't a total loss. This is the original kitchen, though."

As Chloe looked around she tried to imagine her grandmother sitting at the table, cooking porridge and pouring tea.

"Would you like some tea?" the woman asked.

"No, thank you," Nora said. "You've been more than kind, letting us see the place."

"It's quite a bit different I imagine from those days."

"It is," Chloe said. The kitchen didn't fit her grandfather's stories. Chloe tried to sense her grandmother's presence but wasn't able. "Thank you," she said as they left.

"Was it what you had expected?" her dad asked.

"Not really. It was hard to imagine Grandma here. It was too modern."

"A lot of time has passed. You can't expect it to hold still for you."

"No, I guess not. I don't know what I was expecting."

Their Aunt Brigid was being cared for by her daughter, Joanne. Brigid had suffered a stroke the year before and had never regained her full ability to speak. When they explained who they were, she seemed to understand. They had tea with their cousin.

"I remember your mum from the times she visited. I have pictures of you and your sister," she told Jim. "Why did you take so long to visit?"

"Time just got away from me, I guess."

"Yes, time has a way of slipping by and before you know it, you're old. Still, I'm glad you finally made it here." Joanne told them how to find the cemetery where Helen's family was buried. "I would take you myself but I've no one to stay with Mum."

"That's all right. I'm sure we'll be able to find it," Jim said.

"Cousin Joanne, my grandfather spoke of a park where he had first met my grandmother. It was after the war. She was dancing. Do you know what park that would be?"

"I believe I do, but it's not there anymore. They've built over it. But there's a nice park not too far down the street from there."

"That's okay. It was that original park I wanted to see." Chloe tried not to let her disappointment sound in her voice. She wasn't sure what she had been looking for when they came. Some sense of her grandmother's presence. So far she had found none of that.

They visited the graveyard. "Look, Dad, here's the grave for Grandma's brother Jimmy, the one you are named after."

"That it is." Jim looked at the tombstone, 1924-1945. He had just been twenty-one when he died. They walked among the tombstones, looking for familiar names until Mary started to fuss.

"I guess it's time to go back to the hotel," Chloe said. That night they walked along the locks, past where the Titanic had been built and shipped out to sea. As they walked, Chloe remembered her grandfather's stories, how he had walked with Grandma along the water. Was this the same place, she wondered. They had brought some of her grandfather's ashes as well as her grandmother's ashes. He had wanted to make one final trip to Northern Ireland, and so he had.

Something inside her whispered, "This is the place."

She looked for any landmark, any sign that her grandparents had once walked this same spot. She remembered how they had walked along the locks that night when he had come back for her, unsure that she even wanted him; unsure that she hadn't already married someone else. She remembered how they had kissed. She didn't know, but something inside her told her it was here.

"There are thin places," she remembered her grandma telling her. "Places where the veil between this world and the next is thin. You can feel the presence." Perhaps this was one of those thin places. She stopped, taking in all of the feelings, sights and sounds. It was as if over sixty years had slipped away and she was in Belfast in 1951. Something told her she wasn't alone.

"Dad, this is the place. Did you bring the ashes?"

Jim pulled two small bags out of his pocket.

"This is where they kissed after Grandpa came back in 1951. I just know it."

"And if it isn't, it's as good a place as any." He opened the bags and allowed the content of both bags to blow together and be blown by the wind into the locks as they said goodbye.

Acknowledgements

My mother-in-law, Kathleen Magill, was an Irish war bride. Her husband was an American soldier stationed in Belfast during World War II. Eventually she crossed the ocean into America through Ellis Island. Her story was the inspiration for the character of Mary Helen Maguire. This book is dedicated to all the Irish war brides now living in America, as well as the many Irish immigrants who have enriched this country over the centuries.

While only twelve chapters of this book take place in Northern Ireland, they are significant pages that required extensive research on my part. As I posted on my blog – 1,000 hours of research equals two pages of story, or so it seemed at times. There is much I didn't know about Ireland before writing this book, and still more I don't know.

The history of this small island is fraught with violence, a violence that continued through the 20th century, especially in Northern Ireland. When other countries such as India and parts of Africa were gaining their independence from Great Britain, the six Protestant counties in the north remained under British rule, setting the stage for continued violence and warfare. It also set the stage for religious warfare, pitting Protestants against Catholics until the streets of Belfast ran with blood, resembling a war zone, not unlike areas of the Middle East today.

My studies of the history of the IRA revealed that the IRA did not originate as a Catholic organization. During the Anglo-Irish War for Irish Independence, Protestants and Catholics fought together for a free Ireland. The IRA in Northern Ireland resisted being turned into a Catholic organization, seeking joint cause with the Protestants in the North against a common enemy, Britain. However, economic factors at play during that time kept the Catholic population in poverty and out of power, trumping any efforts toward unity. And so, what was a war for freedom, became a religious war and the IRA became predominantly Catholic.

As I reflect further on what I learned about the conflict in Northern Ireland, I find myself looking for ways it compares and doesn't compare to the fighting in the Middle East. Perhaps we can learn from this conflict to help deal with that conflict. Both are situations of long-held differences and hatred. Both have a religious basis, as well as economic factors. In Ireland we have clashes between different forms of Christianity, in the Middle East different branches of Islam. Perhaps we can learn from each.

Despite the history of violence, Ireland played a significant role in civilization. I am indebted to Thomas Cahill for his informative book, "How the Irish Saved Civilization." I also want to acknowledge Tim Pat Coogan for his book, "The IRA," and Ed Moloney for "Voices from the Grave" for information on Northern Ireland during the 1900's. Many thanks to Davy Walsh whose short unpublished work on the history of Ireland introduced me to the topic and gave me perspective. Also to Esther deWall for her book, "Celtic Spirituality" as well as the many websites and other places on the internet with information about Ireland, Irish dancing, language and culture.

Special thanks to my cousin through marriage, Brenda Russell, who shared with me her memories of growing up in Northern Ireland and stories she remembered from her mother's generation.

* The prayer in chapter 11 is found on pp. 30-31 of Esther deWall's book, *Celtic Spirituality*, 1997, Image Books, Random House, Inc., New York

Note to the reader:

Did you enjoy reading this book? If so, please leave a review on Amazon. Your comments would be appreciated and mean so much to me in terms of helping others notice my book. You, the reader, have the power to make or break a book in this day of emarketing and social media.

Thank you so much for reading *An Irish Slip Step*. If you enjoyed this book, I hope you will read others in my Dancing Through Life series!

You can email me, patricia@patriciamrobertson.com or go to my website, https://patriciamrobertson.com. I would love to hear from you.

Patricia M. Robertson

Other Novels by Patricia M. Robertson

Dreamweavers – Dream again, wherever you are in your life.

Buying Time – Visit the peace movement during the Cold War era of Ronald Regan, SDI (Strategic Defense Initiative) and MAD (Mutually Assured Destruction).

Land of Deep Waters - Honduras, land of deep waters, a country torn apart by civil unrest, violence and poverty: Is it possible to go back?

Magnificent Failure - Is it possible to start over? Failures in the eyes of the world and their own eyes, Diane and Jake found each other.

Dancing Through Life Series

Dancing on a High Wire – What do you do when life knocks you off balance? Join Sara, Joy and Esther as each seeks to find a "new normal" and regain their balance on this high wire we call life.

Still Dancing - Some phone calls we love, others we hate, like the ones Pastor Joe receives from his daughter's school. Or the one Dale received at work, letting him know his wife, Joy, had fallen and was in route to the hospital by ambulance. Could her cancer be back?

A Slow Waltz - The road to healing from loss is a slow one, sometimes going backward and sideways before going forward. Sometimes the biggest barrier to healing lies within us. Join Dale, Kathleen, Ava and others as they journey to forgiveness and healing.

Delicious Secrets - A church secretary was the last job Marcie, a college drop-out, would have chosen. She entertains herself with real and imagined secrets about church members until she stumbles upon a secret she would rather not know. Once known, there was no turning back.

About the Author

Patricia M. Robertson is an author, speaker and spiritual director, who is committed to helping individuals find God in their every day experience. She also is author of a companion non-fiction book to *Still Dancing, Walking With Families through the Dying Process*, as well as *Walking with Families through Grief,* a companion to *A Slow Waltz*. She has written other non-fiction books, and writes a weekly blog and monthly newsletter. She has a Doctor of Ministry and over thirty-five years of experience in ministry to families. She currently is enjoying her own love story with her husband, Jack, grown children and grandchildren. For more information about her ministry go to www.patriciamrobertson.com.

Delicious Secrets

Chapter 1

Some secrets are so delicious you just have to keep them to yourself. Like chocolate on a hot summer day, they melt in your mouth. You want to hold them for as long as possible, never giving away to the need to swallow. Their sweetness bursts with flavor. To swallow would be to lose them forever and so you hold on for as long as possible, relishing every morsel.

Other secrets are too good to keep to yourself. They beg to be shared, taunting you, "tell me, tell me!"

And others are meant to be kept silent. They crawl into the recesses of the mind where, if you are lucky, you forget they even exist. There are secrets that in telling cause unnecessary harm. Better to keep silent.

And then there are those that need to be told to clear the air. You have to fight to hold them in. You want to spit them out lest they contaminate the good. You hope that in the sharing they will be robbed of their power.

A family is as healthy as its secrets. I guess the same can be said about a community.

I'm an expert on secrets so I ought to know. I am the holder of the key to multiple secrets, the gatekeeper of secrets. I'm a secretary!

"Is the Sunday bulletin ready, Marcie?" Pastor Joe stood at her desk, Marcie quickly shut the file she was working on.

"Sure, Pastor, ready to go," she said.

"Good. Would you send it to me so I can proof it before we run copies?"

"Sure, only . . ."

"Only what?"

"I've got that thing."

"What thing?"

"You know, that thing. I told you about it last week. Don't you remember?"

"Could you help me out?"

"What good is telling you anything if you are just going to forget? I'll be back by noon. You'll have your bulletin then." Marcie closed her computer and prepared to leave.

"All right. Just make sure I have it on my desk when I return from lunch."

"I'll work through my lunch hour to do it," Marcie reassured him as she picked up her laptop and left. That would buy her some time, she thought. She loved how easy it was to get over on her boss. The fact that he was a minister made it all that much simpler. She would go to the local coffee shop, order a latte and finish her work in the cozy atmosphere. So much more fun than the boring church office.

Joe wondered about his new church secretary. Something just wasn't right, but he couldn't put his finger on it. Is it possible he was being played?

Ever since Edna, the previous secretary had retired, he had been struggling to find her replacement. No one wanted to work for the wages the church could afford. And at thirty hours a week, the church didn't include benefits.

The minute he thought he had a replacement, they would leave for a full-time position with benefits, something he just couldn't provide.

"Sorry, Pastor, I need the hours and benefits," they would explain as they cleared their desk.

"I understand," he said, and he did. The position required someone who considered it a calling, someone who didn't need to support themselves or their family. Someone who didn't need the money. It required a special someone. Someone who knew how to keep him organized, who was discreet, who could be trusted with confidential information. Edna had been that special someone. He wouldn't find anyone like her. At this point he would appreciate anyone with computer skills who actually showed up. He had even tried his daughter, Michelle, in the position, but between school and all of her senior activities, she just couldn't put in the hours he needed.

Marcie was a church member's daughter. He had agreed to give her a shot at the position as a favor to her father. She had dropped out of college and ended up back on her dad's doorstep.

"Give her a chance, Pastor. She just needs to get some direction." Joe had agreed despite his concerns. He didn't want to be the place where wayward young adults got their footing before taking off. He wanted someone he could rely on for the long haul. He didn't want to have to keep training new secretaries. It took time he didn't have, time away from his ministry. He had reluctantly agreed.

"So, how's the latest secretary shaping up?" Kathleen had asked him over for dinner that night. He and Kathleen had been dating off and on for the past year. They had both wanted to keep the relationship quiet, as secret as possible for someone living in the fishbowl of a pastorate. Rather than going out in public, they took turns having each other over for dinner, where they could talk in the relative quiet of their homes, that is, if you didn't count family members coming and going.

"I don't know. There's something not quite right."

"I saw her at the coffee shop this morning, chatting with her friends."

"So that's the thing."

"What thing?"

"Never mind. So, she was playing hooky from work."

"She did have her laptop with her. She was working on something."

"Not church work, I'm sure." She had done a good job on the bulletin though, when he finally got it that afternoon. When she did work she could get a lot done at once. She was efficient.

"Maybe she just needs some direction." Kathleen twirled the spaghetti on her fork.

"That's what her dad says, but this isn't career counseling. I need someone I can count on."

"But it is a church." Joe was aware that Kathleen knew something about needing direction. She had been one such young person. Her misdirection had landed her in prison. "You know, if Joy hadn't taken interest in me, I wouldn't be here." Joy, her sister-in-law, had seen the potential in Kathleen when she had returned home after her jail stint. She had believed in her, given her a chance, given her purpose, direction. Joy had died from breast cancer several years ago. Now Kathleen was in charge of the Arts Center named after Joy, giving her ample opportunity to work with other directionless young people.

"Yes, well, I have enough young people needing direction in the youth group. I don't need another one in my office. If she needs direction, let her get involved with the young adults at church, not play at secretary."

"You know it doesn't always work that way," Kathleen reminded him.

Joe knew. He couldn't argue the point.

"As you always say, God works in strange ways. Who knows why God placed this young woman under your care," Kathleen continued.

Joe had said similar things to Kathleen over the past years. "Touché. Now I see how patronizing those words sound. You've made your point."

"That wasn't my point, however . . ." Kathleen smiled as she sipped her after dinner coffee.

www.ingramcontent.com/pod-product-compliance
Lightning Source LLC
Chambersburg PA
CBHW070952120726
47910CB00004B/1206